THE BRUMBACK LIBRARY
OF VAN WERT COUNTY
VAN WERT, OHIO

A HYDRA WITH SIX HEADS

Recently-qualified Dr Roy Cartwright takes a temporary post as a locum in an established London practice.

Soon, he is falsely accused of the attempted rape of a middle-aged female patient—and the practice receptionist, Lilian, warns him that the same thing had happened to Dr Markson. Now, Dr Markson is reported to be on holiday; but his body is found in Southampton Water.

Dr Cartwright becomes dragged into corruption and he is lucky that his uncle has friends in Scotland Yard who can try to help him. He also has a friend in Lilian . . .

A HYDRA WITH
SIX HEADS

Josephine Bell

BC RY

First published 1970
by
Hodder & Stoughton Ltd

This edition 2002 by Chivers Press
published by arrangement with
the author's estate

ISBN 0 7540 8609 7

British Library Cataloguing in Publication Data available

Printed and bound in Great Britain by
Bookcraft, Midsomer Norton, Somerset

Chapter 1

Roy Cartwright sat back in his consulting room chair, staring out of the window at the untidy remains of a late Victorian garden. Not for the first time in this brief locum he wondered why he had agreed to take on the job.

Well, no, he knew perfectly well why he had come to this sleazy house in an outer suburb of London. Two years qualified, with all the appropriate hospital house appointments behind him, he had chosen most carefully and wisely to take up general practice. He knew his own academic limitations. Not for him a daunting struggle for higher degrees. Not for him, God forbid, the hectic life of the hospital registrars, sweated labour for a scandalously small reward; perhaps at the end of four years no nearer to a consultant post.

He was fully committed to a life in the practice of healing, where healing was possible; in common sense advice; in reassurance; in passing on cases for investigation. He was prepared for the routine, repetitive, boring tasks that went with any job in any field whatsoever, cerebral, academic, managerial, manual. General practice in a group seemed to suggest just what he wanted, provided it was well organised, with reasonable hours of work, reasonable spells on and off emergency duty. The firm of doctors based at Overton near Hythe across the Water from Southampton had come to his notice like an answer to prayer. Until the trouble arose about the date when he should join them.

The advertisement in the medical journal had said, "Wanted immediately. Trainee assistant with a view to partnership." But 'immediately' had meant in a month's time. Hence the locum. Four weeks, actually. Not too far from his teaching hospital; he'd been able to visit friends who were still there, engaged in the rat race he'd left.

What did it matter what the practice was like? At this stage, varied experience was exactly what he wanted.

At first sight the house, 38 Azalea Road, London, S.E. had not looked too bad. Victorian, with steps and pillars at the front door, a dreary, dirty, pinkish-red brick, with dirty grey stone facings, it stood at the corner of Azalea Road and Mafeking Terrace, with its front door in the road. It had been called Spion Cop Lodge when the whole of Mafeking Terrace was built, which dated it and its companion houses there, now mostly turned into multiple flats. Beyond the terrace, where there had been open country at the turn of the century, a big new Council estate provided the solid basis of the practice at Number 38. Azalea Road itself had suffered a large measure of redevelopment, consisting mostly of modern tall blocks of flats with between them the necessary multiple stores, launderettes and other services.

Number 38 had been a doctor's house for over sixty years. The present senior partner, he was told, Dr James Shepherd Williams, having survived the last year of the First War as a young, newly qualified army surgeon, bought the house and practice from a war widow at a low figure and put up his plate. A good deal later Dr Bernard Phillips joined him. There was now a third partner who was taking his annual holiday of four weeks. Hence the locum.

Roy, still staring out of the window, reviewed the three weeks he had spent at Number 38. It occurred to him, not for the first time, that he knew no more of the history of the practice than he had been told, when he was engaged, slowly and with a certain amount of hesitation and digression, by old Dr Williams. Except, of course, that the new surgery, an annexe to the house, with a fresh entrance in Mafeking Terrace, had been built in 1967 and had brought a great increase in the number of patients, hence the necessity for a third partner. Dr Markson had not been with them very long, Dr Williams said, a matter of under two years.

This was borne out by his notes, very sparse, with dates

6

at long intervals, on the National Health Service cards. Roy was sufficiently newly qualified to have kept the good habit of making notes of the condition of his patients and the treatment he prescribed for them. Dr Markson, whose patients it was Roy's job to treat, had neglected this aid to memory and safeguard against all too frequent complaints. Moreover his cases were for the most part dismally uninteresting. Roy sighed, moving his gaze from the shaggy lumps of neglected lawn to the diary where he kept his visiting list day by day. One week more, then perhaps some real medicine for a change.

A knock at his door roused him. He called "Come in" without looking up.

"There are still two patients for you, doctor."

The voice brought him swivelling round in his chair. A charming voice, a charming girl. The old man's niece. The only really bright spot in this dump.

"Patients! The waiting room was empty on time!"

"Private patients. At least Mrs Southport's the patient. Her husband always comes with her."

"O.K. Lil. Has she got a card?"

The girl walked across to a small filing box that stood on the window ledge not far from the desk where he sat. Roy got up to forestall her.

"I'll find it," he said. "You do the formal introduction act."

He himself brought the Health Service patients from the waiting room. But Dr Williams insisted upon having private patients led to the consulting room by the receptionist. In the twenties and thirties they had expected this; even a separate waiting room to keep them away from 'panel' patients. Dr Williams had not come forward with the times. So now his niece went away and came back a few seconds later with Mrs Southport.

She was a thin, discontented-looking woman, of middle age, with a pasty complexion and dull eyes. Roy welcomed her standing, waved her to the chair beside his desk and then sat down, drawing her card towards him and making some show of studying it carefully.

7

It told him practically nothing. Three years previously she had seen the second partner, Dr Phillips. A note in Dr Markson's handwriting, undated, stated this fact but gave no details. So she must have seen Markson too, but he had not recorded this.

"When did you last see Dr Markson?" Roy asked.

"I only saw him the once," Mrs Southport answered, pulling in her thin lips until they disappeared.

"And when was that?"

"I don't see that it matters to you. It's my heart's troubling me now, not the other."

"Which was?"

"Pardon?"

"I just want you to tell me how long it is since you were here last and what illness you were treated for then?"

She gave a short high laugh.

"Treated? D'you call that treatment?"

Roy's patience began to crumble. He was getting used to answers that were no answer at all, but with scorn added, as on this occasion, no progress was possible. He gave up the attempt to extract a history and plunged into the present.

"You say your heart is troubling you. Tell me just what you are complaining of?"

"It's not me so much as my husband. He insisted on me coming."

This road to knowledge seemed to be as securely blocked as the first.

"Have you any pain in the chest? Any breathlessness? Do you notice your heart beating too fast or irregularly?"

"You could say so."

"All of those things?"

"I suppose so."

"Do you ever feel faint or swimmy?"

"I've passed out flat, according to him."

Roy took a deep breath. He was thinking of the list of visits he must get through before lunch. The chances were Lil would have several more lined up for him at the reception desk in the entrance hall of the surgery. There was only one thing to be done. He would consider it necessary in any case. Not because a private patient had to have her money's worth, but because he had to find out what was wrong with her—if anything.

"I should like to examine you, Mrs Southport," he said smoothly, getting to his feet. He went over to the couch by the wall, adjusted the head rest and the pillow, straightened the blanket and folded it back, drew the curtains round to enclose it. "There is a dressing gown on the chair," he explained. "I should like to examine the chest and abdomen."

Mrs Southport opened her mouth to object, thought better of it, gathered up her handbag and disappeared behind the curtains. Roy sat down to make a list of his visits in an order that would save unnecessary driving on the round. He decided to give Mrs Southport five minutes to prepare herself. He still had no idea what she was complaining of, since she had not answered a single one of his questions. But he was determined to go through the normal routine in full, if the only thing achieved was to impress a chronic neurotic with his wish to help her.

At the end of five minutes no word having come from behind the curtains he approached them and asked Mrs Southport if she was ready.

"Thought you were never coming," the sour voice answered.

He went in. The patient was lying back, her legs stretched out, the right big toe, the nail covered with peeling red lacquer, sticking through a hole in her stocking. She was covered by the rug, which she had drawn up to her chin. Her arms were inside it. When Roy took the edge of it to draw it down, Mrs Southport's skinny arms shot out to stop him. After he had removed his hand she turned down the rug as far as her waist, folding her hands across it to hold it there.

"Show me where you feel the pain," Roy demanded.

Mrs Southport waved one hand vaguely above her whole torso, at the same time allowing the rug to slip a little further. She had, unexpectedly, undressed as fully

9

as he needed, Roy thought. In such a patient he had expected to find the underclothes in place needing to be removed or displaced inch by inch. As it was he could get on with the examination at once.

A body as worn, as pallid, as thin and unattractive as the face. No need to feel for the apex beat of the heart; there it was, bumping up and down in the correct space between the ribs, the correct distance from the centre of the breast bone. He spared himself the necessity of laying his hand on that skinny chest to tap out the heart area, but applied his stethoscope directly. Normal sounds, normal beat. He listened carefully, checking with the watch on his wrist. He asked her to sit up and lie back several times. The more rapid beat went back to normal with no marked delay. The lungs too, after careful examination, gave no sign of any disease whatever.

Before leaving Mrs Southport's arterial system to search elsewhere for possible disorder, Roy decided to take her blood pressure. For this he left the cubicle to fetch the sphygmomanometer and as he did so he thought he heard a very faint scraping at his consulting room door. His head was turned the other way at the time, but he spun round and saw, or thought he saw, the door closing softly.

Lil, he decided, wondering if I've made away with the old bag. He strode back to the couch with renewed energy. Mrs Southport whined a little as her arm was compressed but said nothing. A perfectly normal blood pressure for her age.

"I don't find anything in your heart and lungs to suggest a disease in those systems," he said with what he hoped was the correctly impressive tone. "We must try further down—I mean" he corrected, seeing alarm start into her eyes, "the pain you have been having might really be due to—well—indigestion."

"I know what that's like," said Mrs Southport and added, confusingly, "I never have it."

Roy took the blood pressure apparatus away. This time he was not distracted by any noise outside his room and did not glance at the door, though if he had done so he would have seen that it was not quite shut, but held steady with a small open crack. Unaware of this Roy went back to the examining couch.

Mrs Southport lay there with her eyes closed, stark naked, the rug on the floor beside her. Roy had not noticed when she folded down the rug from throat to waist level that she had taken off every single stich of clothing, except her stockings.

"Mad, poor thing," he thought, stooping to pick up the rug. "Scatty as they come. Way up the wall."

He adjusted the covering at hip level, took a good look at the sunken wrinkled yellowing abdominal surface and the two bony hip promontories at either side of it, the bony cage above. With delicate care he tested the reflexes by drawing a finger tip lightly across the surface in four directions. Mrs Southport moaned loudly.

"Tell me if I find a tender spot," Roy said firmly laying a gentle hand on the region of the stomach and beginning to press here and there.

Mrs Southport let out a piercing scream. Roy snatched his hand away but the patient, suddenly maniacal, caught it in hers, dragging him down so that he lost his balance and fell on top of her. Before he could push himself off he felt a large rough hand take him by the collar of his jacket while a grating voice snarled, "You would, would you! I'll have you sent down for assault, s'elp me! Call yourself a doctor, you bleeding bastard! Ouch!"

For Roy, shocked, horrified and bewildered as he was, had managed to twist himself away from his assailant and come back with a punch that would have knocked him down if he had not reeled into the examining couch where his wife was crouching wrapped entirely in the rug she had so recently discarded.

And now another hand reached into the cubicle to pull Roy away and Dr Phillips's voice said furiously, "What in heaven's name's going on here? Cartwright, have you taken leave of your senses?"

The old-fashioned phrase in Dr Phillips's mouth sent a

fresh chill of disagreeable surprise through Roy. He shrugged his jacket into place again and said angrily, "They're both mad. I should have been warned."

Mr Southport, still breathing heavily, left the cubicle and after pulling its curtains together, stood aggressively in front of them as if still protecting his wife.

Dr Phillips said to him, ignoring Roy, "Mr Southport, can you tell me what happened?"

"I heard Muriel scream," the man answered. "So naturally I came in . . ."

"You were outside the door listening," Roy interrupted. "I saw the door opening and shutting earlier on. He's bats," he repeated to Dr Phillips. "They both are. Stark, staring bonkers!"

"Go on, Mr Southport," Dr Phillips said, still disregarding Roy. "You came in and . . ."

"That young scum was in behind the curtains, trying to lay my wife . . ."

"Liar!" shouted Roy. "Bloody liar!"

Mr Southport surprisingly said no more. He simply stood glowering, a hand to his chest where Roy's fist had connected. But while Dr Phillips was turning to subdue his accused locum, the cubicle curtains parted and Mrs Southport appeared, fully dressed, bag, gloves and hat in one hand, in the other a handkerchief which she pressed to her face, but took away again to speak.

"I want to go home now," she said faintly.

Dr Phillips was deeply concerned.

"If you are not too upset to speak of it, Mrs Southport," he said. "I must ask you, for the sake of all of us, to give me an account of this distressing business."

"I want to go home," she repeated.

"Just a word with me first," Dr Phillips insisted. "And perhaps a little restorative."

Mrs Southport brightened perceptibly. She took Dr Phillips's proffered arm and tottered delicately away without a single glance in Roy's direction. Her husband followed, closing the door behind him.

Roy stood for a time staring after them. The whole

12

scene had been staggering, frightening too, in its utter unreality. General practice did indeed have its surprises. He had expected a rather dull routine of minor ailments and up to this day his expectation had been fulfilled. He had hoped for a few interesting cases. After all, hospital practice was always at second hand. The plums of treatment, the final assessment of a disease, were to be found in the hospital, but the start of it all, the first diagnosis lay with the general practitioner. He had dealt with two fractures in the home and one acute appendix. He had located and referred one interesting lump. But there had been no drama. Until today.

And this, as well as being dramatic had also been disconcertingly *melo*dramatic. There was an element in it that he did not understand. Hysteria took many forms, mental illness was always upsetting. But here were two factors he could not accept; or rather that he accepted with an inward shudder. The apparently single aim of the Southports to pin a false accusation upon him. And the astonishing reaction of Dr Williams's partner to the whole situation.

Roy went to his desk and sat down. He decided he had better wait to see Dr Phillips before he started out on his round of visits. For want of anything better to do he wrote on Mrs Southport's record card, in the space intended for the results of his physical examination, the following statement:

Heart. N.A.D. B.P. .35-90.

Lungs. N.A.D.

Abdomen. Examn. interrupted by husband with accusation of attempted rape. Consultation abandoned.

At this point Roy was disturbed by a knock at his door. He called "Come in" and Lilian Bartlett entered, closing the door very quietly.

"Don't ask me anything," she said, coming close to the desk and speaking softly but quickly, "and don't interrupt. Dr Phillips is seeing them to their car. He'll be back in a minute and then you'll be for it. No, *don't* say anything! *Listen!* It's happened before! Same couple. When Dr

Markson was trainee assistant. The *same couple*. The *same scene.*"

She was gone, leaving Roy speechless, doubly, even trebly confused. The melodrama was explained. The collusion. The total understanding between that evil pair. It was an act. But in that case, what about Dr Phillips? What indeed! And Markson had been an assistant before being a partner. Partner in less than two years. Well, why not?

Roy was still sitting at his desk, but staring now, unseeing, at the tangled grass outside, when Lilian came again, knocking loudly, saying in a loud voice from the door, "Dr Phillips would like to see you in his room, Dr Cartwright. At once, please."

As he passed her she whispered, "Don't tell him what I told you!"

He whispered back, "Take me for a mug?" and passed on with a firm tread to the second partner's door, where he knocked and entered without waiting for the girl to announce him.

Chapter 2

At the sight of the locum's red and furious face Dr Phillips rose slowly from his chair. He did not anticipate a physical attack but he meant to forestall any attempt at a verbal one.

"And what have you got to say for yourself?" he asked in the cold, biting voice he usually found successful.

"What have *I* got to say!"

Roy was nearly speechless with renewed fury, but he controlled himself with an effort and went on. "You don't suppose a word of their story was true, do you? Even if the old bag had been a wildly sexy chick I'm not given to passionate love play in the middle of the morning on anything as uncomfortable as an examining couch."

"Facetiousness does not help you," Dr Phillips said coldly, sitting down again.

Roy, following his example uninvited, took the patient's chair beside the other's desk.

"You must know their whole accusation is sheer crap," he said. "Deliberate, criminal defamation of character. I'm not sure I couldn't sue them for it," he said slowly, thinking of Lilian's information. "I believe it was a put-up job. The Medical Defence Union—"

"You listen to me!" Dr Phillips shouted suddenly. "You're more likely to find yourself in the dock than that poor simple-minded couple. Mr Southport swears he found you lying on top of his wife. She swears you told her to take off all her clothes. She was in a state of near collapse. He was threatening to go to the police."

"Let him," Roy said. "She grabbed my hand as I was beginning to examine her tummy. She yelled and pulled hard. I slipped. He was there in no time before I could push myself upright. He caught hold of me and yanked me up, so I pushed him off. I never said a word to her about her clothes. I told her I wanted to examine her chest and abdomen and pulled the curtains round the cubicle. Most women leave their bras and briefs on. She had the rug right up round her. I didn't see she was stripped starko till after I'd finished her heart and lungs and went to examine her abdomen."

"They were very insistent," Dr Phillips said. He had not interrupted Roy's account of the incident and now seemed to wish to play it down without actually agreeing that the young man's story was far more probable than that of the accusers.

"So what?" Roy asked. He was determined not to yield a step in his own defence. "What does it matter? They're not likely to come here again. I suppose they refused to pay their fee? If they don't you can sue them for it later. Or is it better politics to let that sort of refusal slide?"

Dr Phillips's anger rose again at this.

"I've a very good mind to dock their fee from your salary," he said. "You have the impudence to discuss fees at such a time! Don't you realise your position? The harm you have already done to your reputation? Not only as a doctor in terrifying a woman patient instead of advising and prescribing for her—"

"Without an examination, I suppose?" Roy said fiercely. "I'm too new to the job to start the quack system just yet."

It was rude, he knew; it was disrespectful to a senior physician. But Dr Phillips's attitude of suspicion, his readiness to believe false evidence, had brought him nearly to breaking point.

Dr Phillips disregarded the affront. He merely leaned towards Roy and said slowly, "Perhaps you don't realise that you could be struck off the Register for your unprofessional conduct this morning? You say the Southports have no evidence against you? Have you any evidence in your own favour?"

So this *was* it. A frame. Phillips in collusion with the Southports, who had not come here as new patients, as private patients, but for some obscure reason to repeat a dastardly plot. Why? Why?

16

He stared down at his feet, afraid to look at Dr Phillips in case his understanding showed in his eyes. Presently he said, still without looking up, "None, I suppose. Only I would expect you to take my word for what happened, rather than theirs."

"None," Dr Phillips said, now very smooth, even kind. "But I'm prepared to overlook your behaviour in the consulting room and also your truculence to me in here. But there must be no repetition. No further complaints from patients in your remaining time with us. Otherwise I might find it necessary to warn your future employers. In Hampshire, isn't it?"

He took up a letter he had lying on his desk, turning it so that Roy could see it was his own application for the locum. "Yes, Hampshire. Not far from Southampton, I believe. Trainee assistant. They would hardly continue..."

Roy said nothing. An empty threat that would do him no harm, he thought. Until he looked up and saw a gleam of such evil triumph in Dr Phillips's small eyes that he was doubly warned to continue his false submission.

"Very good, sir," he said, his voice suitably unsteady. "I'd better get out on my round, hadn't I?"

"Yes, Cartwright," Dr Phillips said. "You may go. But don't forget what I've said. Your future career depends largely upon your performance in this practice. Your very *careful* performance, you understand?"

Roy nodded. His very careful performance kept his hands down when his dearest wish was to swing a well aimed blow to that pale arrogant face turned towards him. He went carefully to his own consulting room, gathered his bag and his visiting list, looked at the latter to discover where he must drive first and slowly and carefully guided his hired car into the road.

The morning round went smoothly. Several women and children with heavy colds had not developed any complications but were feeling and looking much better. Quite well, in fact. Looking back to his own childhood Roy smiled to himself when he remembered how often his own efforts to avoid school had been unsuccessful, chiefly

17

because the doctor had not been called. His plea that he would infect the rest of his class had been, quite rightly, scorned, since his germ had come to him at school and only the already immune or the lucky had escaped. Of the really ill, two post-operative cases were enjoying their convalescence, which he had no hesitation in prolonging with the appropriate certificates for N.H. benefit and factory excuse. Three frail elderly patients were reasonably comfortable; one more, well set on the way out, was determined to reach his ninetieth birthday and would probably do so by sheer will power. Roy was sorry he would not see this final challenge succeed; the old boy had fought in the first two wars of the century and been a fire watcher in the third; a fighter of one kind or another all his life; very heartening in a world so full of weak-kneed neurotics and twisters.

His easy bitterness faded as he continued the round. Generalisations were stupid; you could always knock them down. Neurotics and twisters got far too much publicity in the mass media. They were a minority of the total population. Except at 38 Azalea Road, it appeared. There was a good deal of twisting there apparently, and he had only a week left to sort it out.

He got back to the surgery annexe at half-past twelve. Part of his duty was to stand by for emergency calls at lunch-time, so he always took lunch there with Dr Williams, who still lived in the old part of the house together with Lilian Bartlett, niece, secretary, receptionist.

The meal was served in the original dining room which had also been the waiting room of the practice in the old days. It was prepared by Lilian with the help of a very faithful middle-aged daily, who had the dignified and unexpected name of Mrs Gladstone. Dr Phillips took his lunch at his own home, a largish corner house at the far end of the new estate in a group of privately owned dwellings beyond the Council terraces and semi-detached houses.

Roy drove into the annexe car park, took his medical bag from the car, locked the latter and went in through the swing doors to his consulting room. He met no one on the way and wondered, not for the first time, why the outer door of the surgery was never locked at midday. The surgery hours were written up outside the building on a large notice and also outside the waiting room, but they were very elastic. More than once he had found a patient sitting patiently, making no personal effort, except his unmoving presence, to announce his arrival. He had been told he could send such people away with a definite appointment for the evening, but usually his good nature and his genuine wish to enlarge his experience brought the unintelligent sufferer into his room. Here, to the latter's angry surprise, after a thorough investigation, he was told to go to the chemist with a prescription for treatment, but without the certificate to get him off work and on to the sickness benefit that had been the sole object of his seeking the doctor's help.

On this morning Roy was thankful to find the waiting room empty. He would have time before lunch, he thought, to write up the results of his visits before the meal. The pile of patients' National Health Service folders was on his desk waiting for him. He had started the system with Lilian in the first week for his locum. He gave her the list of names and addresses before he went out on the round. The folders of notes were ready for him on his return.

So now he sat down at his desk and pulled the small pile towards him. On the top folder he saw a name he knew only too well. Mrs Muriel Southport, 51a Kingsland Mansions, London, S.E. She was registered on the list of Dr Bernard Phillips, M.R.C.S., L.R.C.P.

So not a private patient, to begin with. And in the second place, not a comparatively new patient. Lil had been right. Of course. She was a secretary, wasn't she? And would know. Certainly ought to know.

Then why had she put out, or told him to get out, the private patient's card for him to make his notes on? The card written up by Markson mentioning Phillips but giving no hint of his own findings, no note of any disease at all? Why had Mrs Southport been sent to him instead of to her own chosen doctor, Phillips? Why had Phillips spoken and behaved as if she were a private patient? Obviously all part of the frame he suspected, the object of which was still a complete mystery.

Play it cool, his instinct told him, even when he was on his feet with the folder in his hand, on his way to the door of his room to find Lilian.

He went back and sitting down again pulled out the notes to find what Dr Phillips had to say about this very curious patient.

There was nothing of any real substance. A few remarks about nervous debility made five years ago with a tonic pill prescribed and a mild sleeping tablet to be taken nightly. Nothing more until a brief note, undated, in the same handwriting, presumably Dr Phillips's, which recorded 'Seen by T.M. Satisfactory'.

This must allude to the attendance Lilian had told him of. The other occasion when a similar scene to that of the morning had produced similar results. Again why? With what possible purpose?

Roy shook his head, irritated and half frightened by the crazy fog of suspicion and mystery that was sweeping over him. This folder told him nothing he could usefully employ in his defence, if that ever became necessary. Mrs Southport's duplicity might count in his favour, though he would naturally deny that she had pretended to be a private patient. All the same he had seen the folder and it must have been put out for him by Lilian herself. So presumably she was on his side, or at any rate on the side of truth.

He settled down to making up his notes and when he had finished this chore transferred the remarks he had made on Mrs Southport's private card to her National Health one, dating his account carefully and adding his signature and qualifications. He put Mrs Southport's notes at the bottom of the pile of folders and went into the old house to find Dr Williams, the senior partner of the practice.

Dr Williams did not come to lunch, nor did Miss Bartlett. So Roy ate the usual meal alone, sitting at the large old Victorian dining table in a room papered with dull green large-patterned paper in a Morris design that must have decorated it for at least forty years.

The food was adequate and well cooked, but far from exciting. Roy had been brought up in a family of four children, near together in age, with no complaints allowed at table. Their individual likes and dislikes had been catered for up to a point, up to a nuisance minimum, but not beyond it. He had found this training paid off very well at school and university and medical school. He could stoke up without any emotional obstacles to the process. So now, released as well from any necessity to interrupt his eating with conversation, he got through in half the time, his thoughts far away from his plate.

Dr Williams's absence. Was the old boy ill again? He had missed a lot of surgeries lately. Chronic bronchitis, Phillips said when asked. No, he did not treat him personally. Not a good thing to treat your own partner, any more than your own children. Or your own wife, Roy had suggested and met a sudden blank expression, followed by a chilly agreement and a change of subject.

Well, was this another of the second partner's zest for mystery? Dr Williams had been married and had lost his first wife in the early thirties, presumably after they had been in Azalea Road only about four years. Was there anything odd about this event? No word of gossip, of legend, it would surely be by now, had come his way. But where could it have come from? Not Lilian Bartlett; Lil had not been in the job more than a few years. She had told him so herself.

This thought checked him. A few years, but she knew about Mrs Southport's former visit. Well, the note about it was undated. It could have happened within two years. But no. The note said the woman had been seen by T.M. That must mean Dr Tom Markson, for whom he was acting as locum. Well, did that make any difference? Did he *really* know if this Markson was still in the practice?

21

No one had actually said who it was he was acting for. No, that wasn't true. Lilian had said it when she first handed him folders with Markson's name on. She had let out this morning that Markson had been trainee assistant before he was a partner. Lilian was not hiding anything. Or was she?

He felt he was going round in circles. He must begin again at the beginning. Or rather at the point where he had first seen the Southport N.H.S. folder.

Dr Phillips was the registered name of her doctor. Had he checked the doctor's name on any other folder he had dealt with in the course of the last three weeks? He realised that he had never once done so deliberately. He had accepted the surgeries he had been told to take, five morning ones and three evening. Certainly some patients had said they belonged to Dr Williams. Occasionally these people had complained at not being able to see the old man and had to be soothed and promised a definite appointment with him later, perhaps the following week. A few, who belonged to Dr Phillips, had expressed pleasure at getting a second opinion from someone so fresh from all the latest ideas and gadgetry of a teaching hospital. The great majority spoke only of their aches and pains, their progress or the opposite.

So he really knew very little about the third partner except that he had, on one occasion and this known to Dr Phillips, examined Mrs Southport and the secretary-receptionist somehow knew that the strange incident of that morning had been a repeat performance.

Roy got up and rang the old-fashioned bell beside the fireplace to notify Mrs Gladstone that he had finished his lunch. He waited for her to come, which she did almost at once.

"Your coffee's in the lounge," she said.

He usually took it with Dr Williams in the former morning room, now called the study. The former drawing room, 'lounge' to Mrs Gladstone, was large, chilly and very seldom used.

"Is the doctor out?" Roy asked.

"'E's not well," said Mrs Gladstone with pursed lips.

"And Miss Bartlett?"

"She's with 'er uncle."

"Looking after him?"

"Did'n I just say so?"

Mrs Gladstone was properly upset today, Roy decided. He left the dining room, found his cup of light fawn-coloured synthetic coffee on one of the small cluttered, dusty drawing room tables and carried it to the study door, on which he knocked gently.

It was half opened, after a pause, by Lilian herself.

"Oh no!" she said. She looked pale and worried; her eyes began to fill with tears.

Roy was shocked. Even during the excitements of the morning Lil had kept her calm efficient face and manner. She had helped him with prompt secrecy. She had seemed to him a jewel of a high order in a very tawdry setting and though he had been far too cautious and too absorbed in his first job outside a hospital to consider her as a date or anything approaching it, she had roused his admiration to the point of looking forward to seeing her again.

But not like this. Hampered by the coffee cup, only half empty, he could only put forward a foot to stop her closing the door again and say in a concerned voice, "Is it Dr Williams? Bad again? Can't I help?"

"No," she whispered. "No. I don't want you to see him. You can't..."

But a strange, guttural voice from inside the room called, "Who's that? Is't you, Bernard? Don' stan' there mutter—mutt—ring. Le' um in, Lil! There's goo' girl."

She gave way, hopeless, helpless. Roy went forward, still foolishly holding his coffee cup. The senior partner, clearly stoned, sprawled in his usual big leather armchair. The chronic bronchitis came out of a bottle, then, Roy thought. He might have guessed if he had not been so carefully and persistently trained from childhood to expect those in authority over him, particularly in his chosen profession, to be without vice, even if they were sometimes clearly without brains.

He looked down at old Dr Williams with resignation, though without compassion. He had expected to have a very necessary chat with the senior partner about the case of Mrs Southport. He had meant to get the old boy on his side, stifle Dr Phillip's assumptions, ward off any threat of action by the ghastly pair.

This would not be possible. Another mystery was solved; a full explanation of the senior partner's frequent illness and absence from the work of the practice. The poor old sod was an alcoholic.

"It's Cartwright, sir. The locum."

"The wha'?"

"Locum, sir. One more week. Won't bother you now. I see you aren't, er, very well."

Dr Williams suddenly sat up with surprising ease.

"I am very drunk, boy," he said slowly, carefully. "But I expect that's what you meant. Any special thing you wanted me for?"

"Yes," Roy answered. "But I think it'll keep."

"As you wish. Phillips . . ."

"The trouble chiefly concerns Dr Phillips."

The old man was making a great effort to collect his straying wits. He sat forward, swaying to and fro, until he nearly left the chair for the floor. Both Roy and Lilian had arms out to check the threatened fall. Dr Williams swayed back, belched loudly and shut his eyes.

"Another time," Roy said moving away. But he beckoned Lilian to follow him. She came out, closing the door but still holding the handle, ready to go back almost immediately.

"This is permanent, isn't it?" he said. "An alcoholic. Never quite passes out. Never quite sober."

She nodded.

"And you have to look after him because you are his niece."

"My mother was his wife's sister."

"Was?"

"My parents both died when I was eight. I've lived with Uncle James ever since. And Aunt Emily, at first."

24

She said it all quite calmly, a much repeated statement, Roy felt. He nodded gravely.

"I'm sorry. I've no right to ask these questions. It's just that—well, since this morning I've begun to wonder what sort of a—a practice this really is."

"You have only a week more," she reminded him.

"That isn't the point."

He looked at her as sternly as he knew how, but she returned the look, not impressed in any way.

"It was you looked out Mrs Southport's National Health folder, wasn't it?" he asked, determined to clear up this point at least.

"Yes, I did. Because I remembered from the time before."

"She's on Dr Phillips's list."

"She was seen by Dr Markson once, as a private patient of Dr Phillips."

"She blew her top the same way?"

"Just about. Her husband made the same sort of fuss."

It was extraordinary. Dr Phillips's attitude was unbelievable.

"What happened?" he asked. "I mean, afterwards?"

"Nothing."

"Good God! Nothing! Nothing at all?"

"Nothing at all."

She was gone, slipping quickly back through the door to her useless uncle, closing it very quietly, breaking all contact, shutting Roy out. He cursed her softly and went away to his consulting room to arrange his afternoon round of visits.

Chapter 3

It occurred to Roy that evening that he had now only five days left before he would be leaving his present appointment. He felt that in five days he could go no further in discovering the real nature of that morning's unpleasant incident. Dr Phillips had not spoken to him at all at their chance encounters during the evening surgery. Lilian had removed all the patients' notes he had left on his table. He had intended to take Mrs Southport's folder to Phillips and confront him with it, but the girl had been too quick for that. Too quick and probably too wise. His best plan was to say nothing and wait for any developments that might come. He had, quite unexpectedly, taken the lid off this strange dustbin of a practice. Some putrid remains and a nasty smell had driven him to put the lid back quickly. Let it stay that way.

In the meantime he had five more days, one of them due to him as free time from one o'clock onwards. He still had fixed no lodgings near his new job. He decided to take his time off the next day, drive down to Hampshire, visit Dr Armitage, his new boss and ask his advice about where he should live. Private lodgings would be best, two rooms, if possible. The pub in the village did have a few beds, but would be far more expensive than he could manage on a trainee assistant's salary.

He spoke to Dr Williams about it at dinner that evening. The old man was a little late for the meal but came into the dining room, where Roy was waiting with Lilian beside him and made an easy, smiling apology.

Dr Williams appeared now to be perfectly sober, altogether the former self Roy was accustomed to meet at this meal, affable but serious, anxious to hear Roy's experiences of the day, occasionally producing anecdotes from his own past practice to illustrate any problems the locum was able to put to him.

But the Southport affair was not mentioned, barely approached. Warned by a frightened look from Lil when he tried to introduce the woman's name, he dropped the subject at once. Dr Williams did not attempt to answer the hasty withdrawal.

"But I don't suppose you'd be interested," Roy had said, lamely.

Dr Williams, looking straight ahead of him, might not even have heard this remark. But at the end of the meal, leading the way from the dining room, which Lilian had left a few minutes earlier, he said, "About tomorrow, Cartwright. Did you say you wanted tomorrow afternoon off?"

"Yes, sir. If that isn't inconvenient." Something warned him not to give the whole of his intention. "I go to my new job on Monday next. I ought to take a few things home and see my people about plans before I leave here."

"Home," said Dr Williams vaguely. "Where's that?"

"Near Alton," Roy answered. It was on his way to Southampton and he was not lying. He did intend to take his books and all his loose possessions home from London before he went on to the new practice, because his hired car must be given up before he left Azalea Road for good.

"Alton," Dr Williams repeated. "Near Farnham, isn't it?"

"Fairly near," Roy answered. Dr Williams appeared to be satisfied. He nodded, repeated, "Alton" and moved on towards his study door. Roy was directed to join Lilian in the drawing room for coffee. The old man did not appear again that evening. He had work to do, Lilian said.

Roy attended the morning surgery the next day and then, since he had no urgent visits, set off for the southwest, travelling by cross roads to Guildford and from there by the main road, largely an easy dual carriageway, to his parents' house at Alton where he had lunch and arranged to call in again for dinner in the evening.

It was a fine September day and since it was a Wednesday the roads were not crowded. He enjoyed the drive in mellow sunshine, the fields still covered with golden stubble, though the harvest was all in, the sky the deep blue of early autumn, the chestnut trees beginning to turn. Taking the new road to Southampton he left it to circle the town and reached his destination beyond the western suburbs soon after three o'clock. He drew up outside the house of the principal partner in the practice he was to join the following week.

He did not drive into the practice car park, an area convenient but ugly, snatched from a former wide lawn beside and behind the house. He avoided it for two reasons, the chief of which was the fact that he had not warned his future boss of this visit. His decision to come here had been taken quite suddenly, too suddenly to get in touch with Dr Armitage, except by telephone. And he was now so uncertain, so suspicious of the principals at Azalea Road that he did not trust them not to listen in to his calls. Lilian operated the annexe telephone with extensions to each of the three consulting rooms. There was nothing to prevent her relaying his conversations to the sodden Dr Williams or the aggressive Dr Phillips.

So neither Dr Armitage nor his fat, jolly partner, Dr Thompson expected him and would be surprised and perhaps offended if he walked in on them unheralded. On the other hand he had come down to arrange for a room of some sort to cover at least the first week or two of his assistantship. He had looked for a suitable small hotel or guest house as he drew near the Armitage practice, but had seen nothing except the pub at Overton itself which he had already decided would not do. The houses hereabouts, except that they had large gardens were for the most part contemporary with the original buildings in Azalea Road; turn of the century, red-brick or stuccoed, gabled, wide-fronted, undistinguished, comfortable family dwellings. Quite two miles of them on this road that led circuitously to the New Forest and the sea.

While Roy sat at the wheel of his car holding his AA book open before him as he consulted its map of the area, he noticed three cars turning into the practice car park. Not all at once. They arrived at about five minute intervals. But in one respect they were similar. Their occupants were all dark-skinned or bronzed and all men with the clean-cut features of Asiatics.

From his position across the road and a little behind the entrance this was all Roy could see of them as they drove past him and swung round into the car park. Sea-faring types, he thought vaugely. All nationalities come to Southampton. What interested him more was the thought that their arrival must mean that one at least of the partners was at home, presumably at work. A quarter to four was hardly an hour for visitors. Among women, perhaps, a tea party, such as his mother gave. All the same, unlikely, these days. Very unlikely with only men as guests. No, a surgery. A special afternoon surgery for the convenience of men from ships in the docks. He felt a renewed excitement at the prospect of work among such people.

A few minutes later a young woman came along the road past him, pushing a pram with a solemn baby sitting in it and holding by the hand a lively toddler trying to pull away from her. The young woman stopped just ahead of Roy's car, evidently preparing to cross the road, but finding some difficulty in turning the pram while keeping hold of the tugging child. Fairly frequent cars passed without in any way slackening speed. The girl moved the pram forward once or twice, imperilling the baby and hastily moved it back again.

After watching this while three cars swept by, Roy got out to help her.

"I don't suppose the lad will let me help him," he said, "but may I push the pram over for you?"

She handed it to him without a word. There was another car in the distance approaching at speed which it showed no signs of slackening. They crossed in safety just before it swept by.

"Thank you," the girl said, smiling. "We have a notice each side some way back asking cars to slow down for cars

29

entering and leaving a surgery. But none of them bother."

"You live here?"

"Oh yes."

"I thought you might be a patient. Mrs Armitage, is it?"

Surely not, he told himself. The wife of that tall, dignified, greying fiftyish ... Her sudden cheerful laughter reassured him.

"Heavens, no! My husband's an engineer." She named a big works in Southampton. "We live in the flat."

"The flat?"

"Part of the house is a separate flat. Dr Armitage lives in the rest. And his housekeeper. He's a bachelor."

She laughed again. Roy joined her and then said, as she showed signs of wanting to leave him, "You must think me very rude. But actually I'm coming here to work. My name's Cartwright. I'm supposed to start on Monday and I haven't anywhere to live. I was going to go in and ask Dr Armitage but he seems to be seeing patients—"

His long explanation petered out. The girl wore a strange expression—was it sympathy or disbelief? Or both, interchanging?

He said, desperately, trading on the help he had given her, "I don't suppose you could suggest anyone or anywhere I could get a room? It could be temporary, until I can find somewhere after I've got here."

She pushed the pram further into the drive and let go the walking child's hand. He trotted ahead, moving towards the side of the house. At the same time a man came out of the front door by himself and walked to the parked cars. He was sun-tanned and wrinkled with thick black hair, beginning to show grey wings over his ears; he had deep-set grey eyes. He glanced at the group with the pram but looked away at once, found his car, in which a turbanned Asiatic was sitting waiting, and drove off.

The girl said, "Then you must be the new assistant. In place of Dr Markson."

"Dr *Who?*" Roy said, astonished.

Again the girl burst into pleased laughter.

'*Not* Dr Who. Dr Tom Markson. He left nearly a month ago. Mrs Hurst told me. That's why they're taking on someone else."

Roy swallowed his amazement. The girl must not see it. He must sort this out later.

"Perhaps Mrs Hurst..." he began. "She's the housekeeper you mentioned, I suppose... Perhaps she could help me."

"About a room? Well, I'm not sure I can't. I've just come back from seeing someone... You could try. I know Nancy has a room..."

Roy had an envelope out in a second and a ball point pen held over it. He took down the address. He asked where the house lay. Five minutes walk. Fine. The way she had come.

"I'll try there," he said.

"There's always the Crown," she went on, pointing up the road. "I know they take people in the summer."

"Thanks a lot," he said, beginning to move away. But he came back and said with some embarrassment, "Look, I don't want to barge in on Dr Armitage when he's obviously busy, so I'd rather he didn't know I've been down. I'll tell him later. And that goes for his housekeeper, too. I've never even seen her."

"Haven't you been down to see the place at all?" The girl had her look of disbelief again.

"Of course. Before I took the job. But I only saw over the practice and the books and that. Dr Thompson took me off for a drink at his place. I met his wife. I didn't get that Armitage is a bachelor."

"I see. Well, thanks for your help crossing the road."

"Thank you for this address, Mrs..."

"Pratt. Clare Pratt, Dr Cartwright."

They smiled at one another and he went back to his car, turned it in the practice entrance and drove away slowly, looking for the house of Clare Pratt's friend, who might have a room for him.

A nice kid, Clare Pratt. Friendly, straightforward, countri-

fied. Of course she'd check up on him with Mrs Hurst
and it would get back to Armitage. Couldn't be helped.
But Markson. *Tom Markson.* Left a mongh ago. *Left!*
Then why? . . . He saw a name on a garden gate and drew
in to the side of the road.

Having watched him turn his car Clare Pratt put the
brake on her pram with her foot and searched her handbag for the key to her separate front door at the side of
the house. Mrs Hurst put her head out of the kitchen
window.

"And who's the new boy-friend?" she asked with an
unpleasant leer.

Clare stared, then began to unfasten the baby's pram
strap. The other child carefully climbed the two steps to
the door and stood waiting.

"Good-looking young fellow in the drive just now," Mrs
Hurst went on. 'Saw him from my window upstairs. Had a
car in the road. Or wasn't that his?"

"Oh, you mean the gentleman that helped me cross
against the traffic? Wicked, it is. The notices don't do
any good at all. The doctors ought to get the AA on to it.
Or the local papers. You tell them."

While she was speaking she had pulled the pram backwards up the steps and through the door, which she
shut as she finished speaking. Something to tell Joe, she
thought, laughing to herself. Mrs Hurst hadn't half looked
put out, nosey old bitch. Boy-friend, indeed! What next!

Back in London nothing at Azalea Road had changed,
but Roy found both its situation and the patients who
came to it drearier than ever. But since he had to work
there for only three more full days and since his visit to
the practice near Southampton had been so successful he
decided he could put up with London for that short spell.

Besides, there was Lilian. He had been shocked by her
appearance the morning after his day off. Very pale, red-
eyed (crying or a heavy cold, he wondered) she had
brought him a pile of record folders, put them down on
his desk without a word and was turning away when he
said, "Anything wrong, Lil?"

He had called her Lil since the first week of his locum but he noticed now that she stiffened, though she did not turn round.

"Of course not, Dr Cartwright."

"I'd like to tell you about yesterday—Miss Barlett. I was very lucky. I'm fixed up for a room."

"I'm glad."

She had turned reluctantly. He saw that she really was glad, though she said so little and seemed unable to smile. He was encouraged to add, "I'd very much like to tell you about it. Will you come out for lunch with me today? Get away from here for an hour."

"How can I? Or you, for that matter?"

"I can simply stay away, visiting. Can't you develop an urgent shopping spree or a hairdresser's appointment or something?"

She flushed. Her hair was a mess this week, she knew. There's been no time to have it trimmed. She washed and set it herself. So he felt that way about it, did he, damn him! She put up a hand and made it worse.

"I don't think . . ." she began.

"Please, Lil. *Please.* I've something really very odd to tell you. You'll be surprised . . . I hope."

Her instant look of alarm made him all the more eager to persuade her.

"Look. Meet me in the carpark behind the Odeon at half-past twelve. Invent a lunch date with a friend. We'll go a bit out of this area, but not too far to be back well before two. O.K.?"

"All right. Yes, I'll come. Yes, I'll be there."

Her voice was still hesitant, still reluctant. He wondered if she would come and if not how long he must wait for her if she did not turn up on time. But he need not have bothered. She was exactly punctual for he had only just turned off his engine after parking when he saw her walking towards the car.

She had put on a dress with a jacket to match. The skirt was a good three inches above the knee but not so short that she looked like a heron, stork or flamingo. Not

33

c

ridiculous at all, he decided, admiring the pair of shapely legs approaching him. Her hair, a long dark brown bob, was curling about her neck and shoulders in its usually controlled fashion. Her eyes, no longer red-rimmed, were carefully made up with darkened but not artificial lashes, her lipstick was a delicately tinted pink and did not suggest leukaemia or advanced heart disease.

"You look marvellous," he said admiringly, as he held open the door on the passenger side of the car.

"You didn't expect me to come in my white overall, did you?" she said tartly. Flattery was out, he decided. They drove off in silence.

But at the small Italian restaurant, settling down to a preliminary plate of pasta, conversation began again and flourished as the meal continued. Roy described his journey, his parents, his arrival at his future place of work.

"My father used to teach in a prep school near Alton," he said. "He was headmaster for ten years but he retired fairly early. Now he lives in Alton, so that he can go over and watch the struggles of his successor."

"Haven't you any brothers or sisters?"

"Two sisters. Older than me. Both married. One in Somerset, the other in Yorkshire. My parents make expeditions to visit the grandchildren."

"Lucky you," Lilian said wistfully.

Roy waited. He knew that both her parents were dead, but no more than that. If she didn't want to talk about her family he would not try to make her. But it seemed that she did.

"I was an only child," she said, evenly and without emotion. "And an orphan when I was eight. I don't remember much about our home. It was in Portsmouth. I came to live with Aunt Emily and Uncle James. I've been at Azalea Road ever since, except when I was at school. I was away at school."

"This Aunt Emily was your mother's sister, you told me."

"Did I? Yes, she died six years later."

So Dr Williams was no blood relation, Roy thought. Lil

was his niece by marriage only. This gave him a certain satisfaction, which Lilian was quick to notice.

"No alcoholic genes," she said, smiling sardonically. But her mood changed. "Poor Uncle James," she went on. "He was a very good doctor to begin with, I believe. A surgeon as well as a G.P. He did operations at small nursing homes. Apparently G.P.s were all-rounders in those days."

"Which would be in the twenties," Roy said, remembering. "Yes, I've heard of it. Fairly major stuff, I think. I suppose Azalea Road would have been on the edge of the country then?"

"Oh yes. I used to bicycle out with Aunt Emily to pick blackberries in the lanes. Right up to the late fifties, when they built the Council estate. She used to tell me about the farms just along the road south from us. All gone by the time the war started."

"Then your aunt did not die until—"

" '61. I was fourteen. I'd been with them six years. I was still at school."

"Was Dr Williams still practising surgery?"

"Oh no. He gave that up years before. On account of . . ."

"You don't have to tell me if you don't want to," Roy said gently.

She bowed her head, but after a short pause looked up again and said in the same level, unemotional way, "It got worse after Aunt Emily died, of course, but I was only at home in the holidays, and often staying away with friends. I didn't really know about it until I'd left school."

Roy did some sums in his head.

"Surely your Aunt Emily must have been much younger than Dr Williams?"

"She was indeed. But then she was his second wife."

This time it was clear that Lilian would go no further into family history. Roy went back to his account of his journey to the new practice, his meeting with Clare Pratt and through her his finding of a room to live in.

"Furnished, electric fire, bed and breakfast. Supper on

35

demand," he said triumphantly. "People called Mellish. The husband works in the same place as Pratt. They set up the room for a possible student at the University. It's expanded from Southampton College."

"I know," Lilian said. "Why didn't they?"

"Get a student? I don't know. A bit nervous of the breed, perhaps. Trainee assistant doctor sounds safer, I suppose. Potentially far more lethal, I'd say. Wouldn't you?"

The lunch wound up in an exchange of nonsense. Roy drove back wondering how soon he could take Lil out again. He put her down in a side street half a mile from the surgery and drove back to 38 Azalea Road alone. There was a special afternoon surgery for mothers with young children that he was expected to take. He looked forward to it this afternoon with more than usual sentimental pleasure. He liked children; their diseases could be heart-rending but were, when easily controlled, very rewarding. Children did not cling to their ailments, resenting cure for the loss of importance and perhaps more for the loss of easy money. When children felt better they behaved as if they liked it.

It was not until the last pram had left the car park beside the annexe that Roy remembered he had not said a word to Lilian about the Markson mystery. Never mind, he thought, a good excuse for taking her out again.

Chapter 4

While Roy was clearing up his consulting room at the end of the clinic Dr Phillips put his head in through the door, smiling. He seemed to have recovered completely from his curious attack of suspicion and anger.

"Found your people well I hope?" he asked.

"Yes, thank you." Roy had spent so little time with them he had to search desperately for some way to expand this. He did not want Phillips to think he harboured a grudge or guess that he had been engaged on far more than a visit to his home.

"My father is very keen on gardening these days," he went on, "but he finds the donkey work a bit heavy."

"So you took the place of the donkey," said Phillips, grinning unpleasantly.

"Quite. But it was good to get away from town, if only for the inside of an afternoon and evening."

Phillips nodded. He had been standing in the doorway but now he stepped into the room and closed the door behind him.

"Williams isn't too well again," he said. "He told me yesterday that you'd barged in on him after lunch the day before, when he was one over the eight . . ."

"He was sozzled," Roy said. "He knew it and he told me so. He didn't give a damn."

"*You* don't seem to give a damn either. The point is he won't be fit to take his late night surgeries this week. He asked me to give you a message to take Saturday for him. I shall do his ordinary work tomorrow including the evening but he wants you to take the late night Saturday surgery. Perhaps on Sunday . . ."

"On Sunday I go home," Roy said sharply. "I really finish here midday Saturday. I'm sure you haven't forgotten."

Dr Phillips frowned but did not dispute this statement. He only said, "You'll be here all Saturday, then? So I must ask you to take the clinic. Seven to nine it is, usually. Better take it in Jim's—Dr Williams's room. The doings are all there and cards, syringes, stuff to use."

"How many usually come?"

Roy was well aware that Dr Williams held a registered clinic for registered drug addicts on four evenings a week. This session had been fully used from the night it was set up, which suggested that the addicts, whether registered or not, already knew that Dr Williams would see them and provide their craving with instant relief. This was a side line very far from the surgery the old man had qualified to practice and had given up so early in his career.

"How many?" Dr Phillips shrugged. "How should I know? They're not all junkies. Some are on Jim's poison. I should imagine twenty or so."

"Saturday," Roy said thoughtfully. "I thought that was the evening for your own special surgery, Dr Phillips. Surely up to last week . . ."

"I'm seeing them in my usual hours now," the other answered. "And operating twice a week."

He smiled, his face beaming with smug satisfaction. As well it might, Roy thought. A legal abortion clinic, blessed by the government and all liberal-minded people, with a few hospital strings to pull in the background for the poor or thrifty and a very lucrative small private nursing home with high fees well to the fore. St Helen's. Roy had been over it, with a distraught young woman whose neurotic husband had threatened to kill them all if she went on with her sixth pregnancy. St Helen's was very well equipped. The little nursing home had been established for years, aparently, with a cover front of old people and a surgical theatre doing a fine abortion trade. In those days dire penalties would follow exposure. Dr Phillips had certainly made this limited form of gynaecology his speciality in the practice. But he had no advanced degree, no F.R.C.O.G. However, practice by this time must have made him perfect at the job, Roy thought.

"Tomorrow night, then, in Dr Williams's room, at seven sharp," Phillips said, leaving abruptly.

Roy smiled to himself. Phillips was still sensitive, however legal he had become in his operations. Well, who was he to criticise? His over-fertile patient had been relieved of that dangerous sixth foetus. There would be others like her in the future, no doubt. It occurred to him that the goings on at St Helen's might still be illegal. Wasn't there a rule about the two doctors who could give the signal and actually do the abortion? Not professionally connected with one another and one of them a specialist? He must ask Lilian. Dr Williams had a surgeon's degree. Perhaps St Helen's had always been used in his name.

At seven o'clock the next evening the waiting room was filled with the unhappy, unsavoury, pathetic victims of their own intrinsic weakness. Their special cards were on Dr Williams's desk when Roy went into the senior partner's room to begin the session. Far fewer cards, surely, he thought, than the smelly herd in the waiting room. He knew the rule. He could treat the registered addicts, who were the slaves of cocaine and morphia. He could give them their drugs or compounds in any of their forms. But he was no longer allowed to prescribe these drugs to the unregistered addict. He must record what he did prescribe and write the chits for these issues on Dr Williams's prescription forms that were already stamped with the doctor's name and address, adding his own name and qualifications in the space provided for the principal's signature. He must be extremely careful to keep the prescription block in safety the whole time, as stolen forms were causing a great deal of trouble to chemists all over London as well as to the police.

Roy was quite right about the numbers in the waiting room. Two out of three were not registered. They came to demand, sometimes to beg, for the lesser drugs of addiction. They were not pleased to find a young, intelligent, obviously capable man in place of the muddled, indulgent, white-haired old buffer most of them called 'Dad' to his face. But though many of them protested, menaced, even shouted with rage and despair, at the meagre supplies Roy granted, they were in no shape to offer physical violence. They shambled off, muttering curses and obscenities, with empty threats dissolving into tears as they realised their utter helplessness.

These were the non-registered patients of the practice, whose National Health folders showed their status. Roy gave them small supplies of the drug their notes said they used; too small for them to sell on the black market for the heroin to which they were really addicted. Any visitor who had no record at all at Azalea Road Roy turned away, threatening and blaspheming. After an hour of this crude sorting out the waiting room emptied amazingly fast. The word had gone round. The craving mob hurried away to find another source of relief, a more indulgent clinic or a bent doctor with his chemist colleague prepared to risk breaking the law out of pity or else greed of gain, being paid by hidden pushers.

With the pressure eased Roy was able to give more attention to the patients for whom the clinic was originally opened. The intention had been to regulate their supplies, improve if possible their general health, offer treatment to reduce the intake of the poison that was killing them, attempt a cure. Pious hopes, put forward by warm-hearted souls blindly ignorant of the basic failings of mankind.

Roy, though young enough to have kept some of his early ideals, had no illusions left about the poor wretches who stumbled into Dr Williams's consulting room. They were half-starved and filthy. At least one he found, after a rapid examination, was in a state of advanced lung disease, possibly tubercular, more probably cancerous. He tried to persuade the man to go into hospital. He thought he could get him admitted as an emergency.

"If I go in will they give me my stuff?"

"They'll give you something stronger, I shouldn't wonder. You're ill. Very ill."

"I'm dying," the man said. He spoke slowly, with conviction. Roy had not the heart to contradict him. He prepared an injection, half inclined to increase the dose to a fatal amount to end this appalling suffering.

"Shall I get you a bed as an emergency?" he urged.

"No. I shouldn't like . . ." He glanced down at his rags of clothing; at his feet in the remains of sandals, dirty toes with long black nails. From his speech he seemed to be a man of some education. "Thanks all the same," he said. The injection was already working. He got up, chin in the air, excuse and justification on his lips, cut short by a fit of coughing that sent him staggering back into his chair. He went through the movement of finding a handkerchief that he knew he did not possess. Roy cut him off a piece from a roll of gauze, noticing as the man took it away from his lips that there was blood staining the lump of sputum.

"Hospital," he urged again, knowing it was useless.

"Many thanks, but no," the man said. This time he was able to get up without coughing and walk to the door.

"Writer," he said, disclosing his early dream, his failed ambition. His chin with its weak, straggling beard was up again. "No luck, I'm afraid. Thanks for the advice."

"You've forgotten your prescription," Roy said, walking over to give it to him. "Enough to carry you over the weekend."

Or over the edge, he thought, staring into the dull eyes whose pupils had shrunk now to the pin-points of the text books, giving the man a curiously blank unseeing look.

"I am much obliged to you for your—your unexpected care and understanding," the man said, speaking very carefully and holding out his hand.

Roy took it, unhappily moved, resenting the intrusion of sentiment.

"You'll make a good doctor, young man," the other said. "If I hadn't had this urge to write . . ."

Roy opened the door for him. Poor bloody fool. If he hadn't seen himself a wonder of the world . . .

There were only two patients left now in the waiting room, a young man who got up eagerly, too eagerly, as

Roy looked in, and a woman who waved the young man on.

"He's before me," she said. "I'm not in any hurry."

Roy wondered why she was there at all. She had nothing in common with any of those, nearly all men, who had been in to consult him.

"Come along then," he said to the young man, who seemed to know the way to Dr Williams's room.

"Can you? Please, doctor, can you?"

He was shaking, frantic. He looked very young, still in his teens, Roy decided. He had been a patient of this practice since he was a child of six with measles, according to his notes. Dr Williams was still keeping notes in the late fifties, it seemed.

Roy prepared an injection and gave it intravenously. Both arms were marked with the scars of many injections, some of them badly given.

"If you inject you must use a clean syringe," he said sternly. "Otherwise you risk getting septicaemia, if you know what that is. Blood-poisoning. Dangerous even in these days of anti-biotics."

The boy looked sulky, but said nothing, which annoyed Roy. He didn't look a stupid boy, he was reasonably well-dressed in jeans, a gaudy shirt and an imitation leather jacket.

"I mean it," Roy said. "How did you get hooked, anyway?"

"Exams," the boy said bitterly. "My old man wanted me to go to university."

"But you didn't?"

"Wouldn't mind. They did'n teach me right."

"So you failed the exams and had rows at home?"

"No. I did 'em all right. Had to pep up though."

The pattern was clear. Pep pills to get through the papers. The hard stuff to overcome the depression that followed. Stupid father whose ambition had ruined his son. Or looked like doing so.

"But you're in a job, aren't you?" Roy asked.

"Was. Got my cards last month."

"What was the job?"

"Garage."

"Pumps or repairs?"

"Repairs and that."

"Like it?"

"Not bad."

"Did your dad object?"

"Not 'alf. I got a room now."

As with the last patient this lad's confidence rose as the drug worked in him. He boasted of his independence. He managed to get odd jobs now that had kept him going. But it was clear that he lived poorly, ate snacks at all hours, spent much of his time in small cafés or discotheques with an increasing number of layabouts and small-time criminals. Roy was appalled by Dr Williams's apparent indifference to the decline of a young man who had been his patient from childhood.

"Haven't you got a girl-friend?" Roy asked.

The boy's confidence melted. He had and she had turned him down when he went on the hard stuff. There were others, of course, but . . .

"Don't you want to get off it?" Roy asked. "Get into a decent garage job again? Good pay, regular. If you go on as you're doing you'll be dead in five years."

"Good riddance," the boy muttered. But he broke down after that and declared his real inward wish to have treatment and get back to a normal life.

"That's what this clinic is really for," Roy said, knowing what he said was far indeed from the truth. "For a start you must begin cutting down. Not all at once but gradually. You might force yourself to throw away your syringe and eat this stuff I prescribe for you."

"I'd throw up," the boy said. "I don't eat so much now as I did. No appetite."

Roy was reminded of one important line of treatment that often worked well. Unpleasant, uncomfortable, but dramatic. Only it ought to be administered in hospital. Perhaps St Helen's could cope.

"I'm not going to no hospital," the boy declared.

Roy explained the treatment. It could be achieved by hypnosis or by taking a medicine. In this case, since he was not himself trained in producing hypnosis, it would have to be medicine. Lay off the heroin or take it with the medicine and he would vomit the lot. Following this, eat a good meal with a new tablet he would prescribe. Try it for a few days. Report back—

He realised he would not be there to see the boy at the next clinic.

"You'd do much better in hospital," he said, explaining this.

"It's an idea," the boy answered, having shaken his head again over the thought of hospital. "Say I try it and it works. Dr Williams would go on with it, wouldn't he?"

The more Roy thought about this the less he liked the idea. It was not a treatment anyone could manage by himself. He had been a fool to suggest it. But the boy was looking at him with open hostility.

"Kidding, weren't you?" he said angrily.

"I was not. But you'd need supervision."

"My friend'll do that. You give it me."

Impossible now to go back on his advice.

"Very well," he said. "I believe you honestly do want to stop this suicide lark. You must promise me you'll stay in tomorrow and follow my instructions. I'll tell Dr Williams about you. Come back here on Monday. You'll need a new prescription by then. Whatever you do don't try to inject any of the things I'm giving you."

"O.K." the boy said. He took the prescription form and went away.

Roy went to the waiting room to bring in the last patient, the woman he had seen sitting there, her head bent over a very out-dated magazine. He met her walking across the room towards him.

"Why, Mrs Gladstone, I didn't recognise you!" he exclaimed.

"No, sir, I don't suppose you did."

He stood aside for her to go ahead of him and waited until she had settled herself in the patient's chair. He then noticed that the last folder of notes before him on the desk was indeed that of the daily cook-housekeeper. He pulled out the record pages. There had been nothing written there for the last three years.

"You'll have to tell me what Dr Williams is treating you for," he said. "I'm afraid he hasn't put it in your records."

He looked at her in some alarm. Dear old Mrs Gladdie a junkie? Surely not. But if not why sit in there with all those jerks? At this time of night, too!

Mrs Gladstone read his anxiety in his young good-looking face. She laughed aloud.

"None of your so-called trips for me, dear," she said. "I'm not such a fool at my age. If you ask me it's just a silly fashion and them that encourages them. Wicked bastards."

"Then what . . . ?"

"Dr Williams gets me to sit in there just in case any of them gets a collapse or turns nasty. We don't want a panic or anyone roughed up in a set-to of any kind."

"But what could you do, Mrs Gladstone, if they did turn nasty?"

"Give them a piece of my mind for a start. If that wasn't enough and they hippies is mostly chicken, I'd call the doctor and if he couldn't stop it we'd have the fuzz in. But we wouldn't go to that length if we could 'elp it."

Roy nodded. The evening had been an eye-opener and one that had been kept pretty carefully away from him until this last, this very last, opportunity. Why?

He looked again at Mrs Gladstone's notes, turning the cards over and back to read the few sporadic remarks recorded there. One cryptic line, 'To St Helen's. Contact Bernard.' Five years ago.

"You were under Dr Phillips in St Helen's at one time," he said and waited. "But that was a long time ago."

"Dr Phillips got me out of my trouble," Mrs Gladstone said, quite calmly. "That was how I come to work for them 'ere. To pay the fees. It's different now," she said,

45

"or I wouldn't be letting the cat out of the bag to you, young man."

"You mean the fees?" Roy asked, deliberately mis-understanding her, "or your ability to pay them? Both, I expect," he added, smiling openly at her.

She had expected his disapproval, had half-hoped to shock him, at any rate to test his ability to make his innocent way in a wicked world. She leaned forward and began to speak in a lower voice.

"Dr Cartwright, it's been a pleasure to have you 'ere these few weeks. Miss Lilian is going to miss you, bless her poor little heart. Things is not what they should be, as I think you've noticed. Poor Dr. Williams. Never been the same since she died. Times he can't control it at all. Like just now."

"I know," Roy said. He began to feel a rising excitement. Mrs Gladstone had served this ropey practice out of loyalty for risks taken on her behalf as much as from a determination to pay the price for them and for her own previous indiscretion. She was trying to tell him about it. Why? To inform him or to warn him? He waited. He did not know how to encourage her to further revelations but he had already learned the general practitioner's first lesson, to listen without interruption and then try to put some order in a mass of apparently unrelated facts.

"Not that I saw much of 'im before I come to work in the house," Mrs Gladstone went on. "I do remember the lady, though. Very well spoke of. Dr Phillips wasn't in the practice then, but I knew the lady that was cook, living in. There was another doctor that left to go to Canada. Then there was Dr Smith, poor man. Friend of Dr Phillips."

"After you came here, then? As well as Dr Phillips?"

"About three year back. Yes, after I come."

"What became of Dr Smith?" Because he must have left after a very short spell if Tom Markson had had a turn-up with Mrs Southport about eighteen months or two years ago . . . undated, the note about it. Mrs Gladstone was speaking, still more softly.

"He died, poor gentleman," she said. "Overdose. Accidental, they brought it in. It wasn't, sir. He'd got to be taking those things regular. They couldn't stop him, so he died."

"How long had he been here?"

"Just over a twelvemonth. It's my belief he was hooked as they call it before he come."

"And then they found Dr Markson?"

Mrs Gladstone sat up straight, her mouth working. "They've never . . ." she began, but Roy stopped her with a question.

"Don't ask me how I know," he said, "but I do. Not how they found him, but how, not so very long ago, he had—well—an experience with a patient belonging to Dr Phillips. The doctor knows that I know this."

Mrs Gladstone thought for a time, then she sat forward again.

"That settles it," she said. "You was told you was locum for our Dr Markson, on holiday for a month?"

"That's right."

"I can tell you Dr Markson has not been on holiday. He's been working this last month for a couple of doctors in Hampshire. Near Southampton."

Roy stared. A chill spread through him, a chill wave of suspicion, unbelief, fear. Mrs Gladstone nodded, rose, pressed a hand on his shoulder and walked out of the room.

Chapter 5

When Mrs Gladstone had gone Roy sat for a time thinking. Matters were more serious than he had thought, than he could ever have imagined when he accepted the position in Hampshire and then arranged to fill in time here in Azalea Road. According to Mrs Gladstone there was a very definite connection between the two practices. Through Tom Markson, who seemed to have a foot in each, unless there were two Marksons. But no, the activities of this mysterious doctor in his apparently double role seemed to dovetail quite easily without having to supply him with a twin or double. How then could he possibly have come to engage himself with both practices? Dr Armitage in Overton had not mentioned Azalea Road. In fact when he had first applied to Armitage and gone down to visit the place and be interviewed he had not considered taking any job at all to fill the expected interval. What had made him take the locum, then? An advertisement? It must have been that. In which medical journal? He could not remember until suddenly he thought of his Uncle Harry.

He had called in at his home on his way back to the hospital in London at which he was finishing the third and last of his six-monthly house jobs. Uncle Harry was visiting his parents, kind and clever as usual; very interested in his plans for the future. It had been Uncle Harry who had sent him a cutting from a news sheet or journal inviting applications for a locum in a three man practice at 38 Azalea Road, S.E., together with a short note that merely said "This do?"

It had seemed to do admirably for three weeks. Now it did not 'do' at all. Everything about it had in three days become unexpected, confused and most alarming. Even

Uncle Harry's kindly assistance was suspect. Well, that at least was easily put straight.

Leaving the addicts' records in a neat pile on Dr Williams's desk Roy went out of the room, locking the door behind him. The annexe doors were always kept locked at night and the windows protected by substantial shutters behind stout bars. The connecting door from the annexe into the house was also locked and the whole building fitted with a burglar alarm. When he took out the last key Roy switched on the alarm. It amused him to remember the casual way the annexe was treated during the day compared with all this night care.

He found Lilian in the drawing room, reading. He poured the keys into her lap.

"Ready for your snack?" the girl asked. "Coffee, cocoa, beer, whisky?"

"I'll get it," Roy said. "Yes please. Ravenous. Flaked out. *Addicts!*"

"Sit down," she said. "I'll get it. Soda or water?"

She was on her feet, passing him. He put an arm across her shoulders which stopped her dead.

"If I sit now I'll be asleep in ten seconds flat. And I've got a call to make. No, telephone, not patient. I want an outside line by myself, no extensions."

She moved away from his arm, only saying, "You'd better come with me. I'll show you, then you can't blame me if anyone knows what you say."

"Your little office is bugged, is it?"

"I think so, but I know this room isn't. May I know who you want to speak to? I mean is it a trunk call or what?"

"It's a family number—in London—you can deal with it for me if you like. My Uncle Harry."

She went with him to the end of the hall, to her tiny office that had once been a parlourmaid's pantry. She adjusted the small telephone exchange to give him an outside line and then left him.

Uncle Harry was at home. He accepted responsibility for suggesting the locum but without regret for the outcome. On the contrary he appeared to be delighted.

49

D

"You leave London tomorrow, do you?" he said, eagerly. "I want to hear a lot more about it that you may not like to tell me over the phone. Going down to Alton for the night?"

"I wasn't. But I think I will, now, as things have turned out."

"Come to lunch first. You can get to Alton for tea. You won't go on to the new place till Monday, will you?"

"I'm supposed to start work there on Monday. If I go at all now."

"Of course you must go. That's all right. Lunch here, tea in Alton, new digs at what-d'you-call-it for supper."

"I'll come for lunch. Thanks a lot. But I can't stay long afterwards."

"Come early then."

"I'll try."

It had always been difficult to refuse Uncle Harry anything he chose to demand. Mainly because he came up with such marvellous presents at one's birthday and at Christmas. But also because he had that practised lawyer's manner, the barrister's skill in finding instant argument to beat you down or in another context drag knowledge from you by force of manner or lead you gently into lethal legal traps.

Roy hung up, no more informed than he had been, but with a definite hope of enlightenment the next day. He went back to the drawing room. Lilian was there with a trolley holding plates of sandwiches, biscuits, cheese and fruit. Dr Williams, in a dressing gown, pale but seemingly quite sober, was there too.

This was unexpected, but fortified by Mrs Gladstone's revelations and his uncle's invitation with its implied support, Roy said at once, "I'm glad to see you're better, sir."

"Yes," Dr Williams answered. "Lilian tells me Bernard got you to take my addicts clinic. A painful chore, as no doubt you found it."

The old man's face was stern, his voice did not suggest

the gross hypocrisy Roy suspected. A wave of anger swept through him.

"Painful and disgusting," he said. "They only come for supplies, don't they? They seemed to resent any suggestion of finding a cure."

"Did you offer them the hope of one?"

"It wasn't possible with most of them, even to suggest it. There were far too many. I'd have had a riot on my hands if I'd taken enough time with each of them to attempt any real advice, let alone treatment."

"Exactly." Dr Williams gave him a very steady look. "You realise, of course, that mine is a registered clinic and therefore licensed to issue the hard drugs which the general run of G.P.s is now forbidden to prescribe to addicts."

"Of course. But the general run of the G.P.s don't have drug addicts on their lists. They refuse to have them unless they undertake to go for cures."

"Very high-minded and time-saving," said Dr Williams. "Short on compassion, don't you think?"

Remembering his ill-advised attempt to help the desperate boy in the surgery Roy said, "I don't know how you'd really begin on it, but I know I couldn't stand for long just dishing out the poison."

Dr Williams sighed.

"You have much to learn, young man," he said. "You could start by not frightening the life out of our private patients."

Roy was astonished.

"Do you mean that hysterical woman, Mrs Southport?"

"I do mean Mrs Southport."

"Then all I can say is you've got it wrong right through. I did nothing whatever to frighten her and she is not a private patient. She is on Dr Phillips's list and I think .the whole exercise was a put-up job, though I can't imagine what the object was."

Dr Williams glared. His whole frame began to tremble. Lilian sprang to her feet.

"You've been up quite long enough, uncle," she said

quickly. "Come along now. It's getting on for eleven. Don't forget Dr Cartwright is leaving tomorrow."

The old man, who had obediently been getting to his feet, put out a hand to grasp his niece's shoulder while turning to face Roy.

"Leaving?" he said vaguely. "I thought..."

Lilian beside him made frantic signals to Roy, so he merely said, "Goodnight, sir" and went to the door to hold it open for Dr Williams and his escort. He waited half an hour for Lilian to come back but she did not do so. He poured himself another drink and when he had finished it, took himself to his own room.

He no longer felt tired. The clinic had exhausted him both mentally and physically, but chiefly in his emotions, where a thick greasy blanket seemed to have been drawn over his spirit, blacking out his normal view of mankind, his normal wish to set right the results of normal accidents, to fight the inevitable encounters with those normal competitors for life, the microorganisms, to correct normal faults in the mechanisms of the body and mind. His pity had been tested too far. Whatever weakness or stupidity had started the rot in these victims the process could not now be reversed. He remembered a rat he had once found at the bottom of the garden in a trap, a cage in which the bait was suspended from a hook that worked the door of the trap. The rat had taken the bait so greedily that the hook had pierced the roof of its mouth at the same time that the cage had shut. So the wretched creature was held in agony until he had come upon it. He was twelve at the time. He had fetched a bucket of water and dropped the trap into it and left it there. He had not wanted to tell anyone about it, he was so sickened by the whole episode. But his white face betrayed him to his mother. In due course the bucket was returned to the house and no more rat traps were laid at the bottom of the garden.

These trapped addicts gave him the same sort of sick feeling, of helplessness at their greedy embrace of a slow painful suicide.

The blanket of despair did not lift. Roy knew that if he went to bed at once he would not sleep. Other matters, notably the mystery of Dr Tom Markson, would crowd in to replace the horror of the addicts.

He snatched at the one cheerful aspect of his immediate future. Lunch with Uncle Harry. As early as possible. So he needed to pack. Pulling his two suitcases from the top of the wardrobe he settled down to filling one of them with his clothes and the other with his remaining books and various small oddments he had acquired during the last four weeks. He was thankful he had been wise enough to take all the heavy stuff and most of the books to Alton on Wednesday.

When he had finished and the drawers and cupboards were empty he decided to go downstairs to see if he had left anything of his behind. It was after midnight. The house was very quiet, quite deserted. He supposed Lilian and Dr Williams were both in bed and asleep.

He turned the landing light switch as he passed. It operated another light at the turn of the stairs where another switch produced a light in the hall. Before he had gone down the last few steps of the staircase the front door bell rang loudly and continued to ring.

Roy stood still at the foot of the stairs. Emergency calls in this neighbourhood came by telephone. At nearly half past twelve a casual appeal for help was unlikely. There were two main possibilities. The police with a walking casualty picked up in the street or an addict so far gone he no longer knew the time of day, but only that his supply had run out and Dr Williams was kind. As this was a day when the legitimate clinic operated Roy considered an adddict the most likely customer.

He went to the door, which was fastened by a Yale lock and a chain halfway down. He undid the lock but left the chain in place and opened the door a few inches.

"Yes?" he asked the two figures standing outside. Both seemed to be men, one wearing a battered hat, the other a bush of frizzy hair. They did not speak but pushed forward against the door, which being heavy and Victorian neither cracked nor bent but came up against the stout chain with a jar that sent them both reeling backwards. As the light of the nearest street lamp fell on them Roy recognised the frizzy bush.

"You came earlier tonight," he said, pointing at the man. "Why have you come back?"

"You gie me ... You gie me ..."

Roy turned to look at the other man.

"You Cartwright?" this one asked.

"I'm Dr Cartwright, yes."

"You give 'im a dud paper. 'E 'as supplies give 'im for two days."

"I gave him the right amount for two days."

"Chemist said you give no more than 'e 'anded out. They'se gone now. The lot."

"I'm afraid that's not my responsibility."

"It's bloody well going to be."

Something that looked very like a pistol appeared in the thug's hand.

"I have no prescription forms in this part of the house," Roy said, edging in behind the door. "You've come to the wrong door, mate."

"We don't want forms," the addict whined. "We want the fix. Dr Williams always gie's me ..."

"Dr Williams is in bed. He's ill. I told you that before. All the medicines are in the dispensary in the annexe."

The pair seemed to retreat down the steps. At any rate Roy felt the pressure on the door relax. He stood away from it, collected his strength, flung himself forward and slammed it shut, pushing down the catch on the Yale lock. Then he sprang away to Lilian's little office to telephone for the police.

The office door was locked. He dashed upstairs to the extension in his room. There was no dialling tone. Incoming calls were not for him that night, then.

Why? Because he was leaving the next day? Who would get them? Presumably Dr Phillips. Only it was usual for whichever of them did evening work of any kind to continue on duty until the morning.

He did not stay upstairs to think this out. He was already running down again, to pick up the annexe inside door key from beside the letter rack in the hall. There was a telephone on the reception desk there. Surely that would be working. It occurred to him as he went through the connecting door to wonder why the key to Lilian's office had not also been hanging up near the letter rack.

The attack came just as he was picking up the receiver. He did not remember afterwards if that telephone, too, was dumb. He heard the rush, clumsily performed, in time to swing round and duck. So the blow landed on his shoulder putting his left arm out of action for a few minutes. But his right caught the hatted thug behind the ear and sent him sprawling. He swung round further to take the self-styled addict's boot on his upper thigh, saving his groin, His own foot hooked the kicker's supporting leg from under him so that he fell beside his friend. Roy had time to jump the reception desk, seize a heavy paper weight he found on it and prepare to hurl it at the first of the two to rise.

He very nearly threw it at Dr Phillips, who at this moment appeared from the darkness of the waiting room, tall, dignified and very angry.

"What in hell's name goes on here?" he yelled at the top of his very powerful voice.

For Roy this was positively the last straw. His blood was up, his success in battle so far made him eager for more. He shouted back, "What the hell are *you* doing here? To let these lousy thugs in?"

Dr Phillips turned to the two who had now struggled to their feet.

"Get out!" he said fiercely. Without a word or a look in Roy's direction they slouched to the outside door of the annexe and disappeared.

"And now perhaps you'll tell me what's been going on?" Dr Phillips demanded.

Roy put down the paper weight. His left arm would bend at the elbow now and feeling had returned to the hand. He supported this with his right hand, though the knuckles of that were now swelling and two of them were raw. He described the visit of the two men.

"You had not gone to bed, I see."

"I was packing. You may remember I leave tomorrow."

Dr Phillips ignored this.

"When they threatened me and I managed to shut them out of the house I wanted to call the police. But Lil's—Miss Bartlett's office was locked and the key gone. That was why I came in here to see if this one was working."

He stretched out a hand to the receiver but Dr Phillips stopped him.

"I wouldn't if I were you," he said. "I think you'll be hearing from them any minute now."

"What d'you mean?"

But he thought he knew only too well and his fighting ardour evaporated in that instant.

"I had a call from them myself," Dr Phillips said with obvious satisfaction. "Two calls, to be exact. From Mills, the chemist, who had been visited in connection with various prescriptions you issued this evening and later from the local station who had taken in as drunk and disorderly a youth they found vomiting over a railing near the park. Only it wasn't alcohol he'd taken."

Roy groaned.

"I told the silly blighter to follow the treatment at home," he explained. "He was genuinely anxious to get off the hook. I believed him when he said he'd do anything except go into hospital. Well, you know what hope there is of placing any of them, unless they're in the last stages, incapable and all that. I ought to have made sure he knew what he was doing."

"He knew all right. He cashed your prescription, went to the nearest cafe and ate the lot."

"My God!"

"Exactly. A constable called an ambulance and the ambulance crew knew him as a junkie. He was just able to say what he'd done before he started throwing up again.

They got the chemist's name and through that on to me."

"Why you? The prescription forms were Dr Williams's."

Dr Phillips did not answer this question. How many of the local chemists played in with him, Roy wondered. He blamed himself for not insisting on the wretched junkie going to a real hospital for real treatment. But actually he had not over-prescribed nor given anything he shouldn't. So the police had nothing to see him about, far less charge him with any legal irregularity.

He began to feel very tired. His head was aching, his shoulder hurt where the thug's blow had fallen. The joint had stiffened, it was painful to move his left arm at all. When he turned to walk away his thigh protested so sharply that he let out a cry followed by a curse.

It was then that he saw Lilian. She was standing in the shadows beyond and behind Dr Phillips, in a long dressing gown over wide-legged, filmy pyjamas. She now hurried forward, concern on her pale face.

"They hurt you!" she exclaimed.

"Less than they meant to," he answered, limping on towards the inner door.

Dr Phillips, scowling worse than before, said, "I advise you to wait for the police, Cartwright. This could be serious for you in your new job."

Roy swung round.

"I don't think so," he said. "I don't believe the cops are interested in me at all. I don't believe they'll come here, because if all you've said about that young junkie is true, I'll bet you've squared the law with some other tale. It won't be the first time. Don't worry about me. I can look after myself as and when and from whom the attack comes."

Dr Phillips did not move. Lilian came to his side, whispering, "What did they do to you?"

When they had left the annexe Roy said, "You knew about those types? Phillips set them on me, didn't he? What does he want? What's the point of it all?"

She answered only the first of his questions.

"I knew there was some sort of fight over there." She

jerked her head towards the door they had just come through. "My room is at the side of the house above where the annexe joins on. I came down to help."

"Me? To help me? How did you know I was involved?"

"Well it wasn't Uncle James. Your room door was open and the light on and you weren't there . . ."

"I see. But Phillips was there too. Wonderful timing, I must say."

"Lilian!"

Dr Phillips was there behind them, beckonging to the girl. "Don't . . ." Roy began, but she turned away, dignified, cold, moving quickly away from the hand he had laid on her arm.

"Yes, Dr Phillips?"

"Come here."

She went back without another word. Dr Phillips opened the connecting door for her, then followed her, closing it behind him.

Slowly, painfully, raging at his helplessness, at his inept flounderings in the mud of this unsavoury pactice, Roy made his way to his room, undressed with difficulty and at last managed to crawl into his bed, where in spite of his bruises he fell almost instantly into a deep sleep.

Chapter 6

Roy was woken at eight o'clock by the telephone ringing at his bedside. The answering voice was Lilian's, on the house phone.

"If it's an emergency put it through to Phillips. Say I've left," he instructed with a sense of pleasure.

"It isn't. It's me asking you what you want for breakfast and when you'll be down. You said you wanted to get away early."

"So I did. Ouch! Sorry, that was my shoulder. No, it works, but doesn't like it. Sausages, if you've got them. I'll be down in ten minutes. No, I'll be slower than usual. Give me twenty."

In the end he took half an hour because he decided to soak the painful shoulder in a hot bath and follow this with a careful shave. He wondered if the Mellishes at Overton had a point in his future bedroom suitable for his electric razor. He hadn't asked. There were many things at Overton, both in the practice and his digs that he hadn't asked about. In fact he was beginning to think he'd been a proper Charlie over this bloody locum and everything that went with it.

He got to his breakfast at last in a state of profound disillusion and disgust. But four stout sausages and two large cups of coffee did much to restore him. He was even able to notice Lilian's continuing pallor, the dark rings under her eyes, the way her lips trembled when she did not keep them pressed together. But he remembered how she had appeared the night before in the annexe and how she had obeyed that bastard, Phillips, without a word.

"Have you had breakfast already?" he asked, hating the abyss that seemed to have opened between them, but determine not to ask questions he knew she would refuse to answer.

"I'm not hungry," she said. "More coffee?"

"Only if you'll join me."

"Yes."

She refilled his cup and poured some into another for herself. His defences crumbled. He leaped the gap between them.

"You've got to get out of here, Lil," he said, putting out his right hand to cover her left where it lay on the table beside her empty plate. She left it there but turned her face away from him.

"I can never leave Uncle James. I promised Aunt Emily before she died."

Roy frowned.

"Wasn't that a terrible burden to put on you? Only fourteen wasn't it?"

"You remember that? Well perhaps. But she was so afraid for him. And then—well, she may have thought he wouldn't live very long."

"But they do, you know." Roy was suddenly professional. "It's supposed to poison their livers and kidneys but it takes a hell of a time to have any appreciable effect."

Lilian was smiling at him. He laughed.

"Text book only. Your point. You know too much, my girl."

"I've had time."

"Far too much time." He pressed his hand on hers. "I may not know much medicine yet, but I have enough common sense to know things are pretty lousy in this practice. Oh, the stuff they gave me to deal with was all quite O.K., the usual general practice with a fair number of interesting chronic cases to follow up from their hospital investigations. Dr Williams, what's left of him, can still hold them. He must have been good in his early days."

"I'm sure he was. I think Aunt Emily married him as a rescue operation. Only it didn't work."

"They say it hardly ever does." Roy paused. He did not want to discuss Dr Williams, but his vile partner, Phillips.

"When did Dr Phillips join the practice?" he asked at last.

Lilian drew her hand gently from under his. She got up, beginning to gather the dishes together. Roy got up, too.

"Don't run away, Lil." He had his arms round her now, pulling her gently away from the table. "Darling Lil, don't run away from me. You see, you've got to run away from *him*. You've *got* to. He's dangerous."

For a moment she melted in his arms and turned to him and pressed her face against his shoulder. Unfortunately it was the injured shoulder, so that he let out a sharp yell of pain and the promising situation exploded into curses, apologies, retreat, anger, protest and finally, because they were both young and mutually attracted, wild laughter.

Roy recovered first.

"He seemed to think he could order you about," he said obstinately. "The drug clinic here is obviously phoney, I should say, illegally and therefore criminally phoney. St Helen's is nothing but a one-time abortion hide-out."

She shook her head but said nothing. And though he argued with her until she had filled her tray and pushed it through the service hatch into the kitchen, he could not persuade her to tell him anything about the bent Dr Bernard Phillips or his crooked schemes.

Only when he had finished his packing and brought his bags down into the hall, she came to him again with a message from her uncle.

"He's up and in his study," she said in a low voice. "You must say goodbye to him. Don't tell him about last night—the row, I mean. I think he knows. Bernard—Dr Phillips has probably told him."

Roy went to the study. Dr Williams, white hair very sleek, beautifully brushed, dark suit, well brushed, was sitting at his desk.

"Come in, Cartwright," he said. "Sit down."

Roy approached the desk, but remained standing.

"I have to get off," he said. "I have a personal call to make in London before I leave for Overton."

Dr Williams held out an envelope.

"Our final settlement," he said. "Including overtime."

"Overtime?"

"We pay our locums generously, my boy. The usual standard fee per week, but we always add something for late night calls or visits and clinics after the usual hours."

Roy stared. Dr Williams stared back. Roy started to open the envelope, but the old man stopped him with a wave of his hand.

"Not now, not now. Send me on a receipt if you like. But it's a cheque so there's no necessity for you to waste a stamp." He struggled to his feet. Roy noticed that the effort made him breathless. "Goodbye, Cartwright and good luck in your new practice. Take your principals' advice at all times. Avoid—well, we'll say no more."

He held out his hand. Roy took it with reluctance. He had begun to feel sorry for the old man, but not now. Old hypocrite—old scoundrel. As bent as his evil partner seemingly. He murmured a few words about the value of all kinds of experience. Let him take that any way he damn well likes, he thought, as he left the room.

Lil was no longer in the hall when he picked up his luggage and went out to find his car, but she had opened the garage and was waiting there.

"Don't you have to give up this car?" she asked. "How will you manage? By taxi and train?"

He would have explained his plans but he was still annoyed with her for refusing to discuss Phillips.

"I'll manage," he said. He arranged his bags on the back seat, reversed the car into the road, empty on the Sunday morning. But when it came to leaving her, he found he could not do so in this way, rudely and abruptly. He got out again to go up to her and put his sound arm round her.

"Thanks for everyting," he said. "I'll keep in touch—if I may."

"Oh yes. Oh, please do." She was gentle and breathless now. He kissed her cheek gently and seeing her mouth tremble again as it had at breakfast, kissed it firmly before he left her.

"Be seeing you," he said, as he got back into the car.

Roy's uncle Henry Killick was a barrister, a Q.C. with a

special interest in criminal cases. He lived with his wife Rachel in a pleasant house in a Kensington Square not wholly given over to multiple dwellings. The former basement kitchens of the Killicks' house had been converted into a separate flat with its own front door in the area. Even so, the house was clearly too large for the couple's everyday needs, but they had, like Roy's parents, two daughters married with young families and living in country towns not more than fifty miles from London. This meant frequent visits at weekends, when the old nursery came into its own again. Rachel baby-sat with indulgent pleasure while her own children took evenings out at theatres or concert halls and were spared for short spells from the endless round of cooking, cleaning and jobs about the house.

As Roy drove into a deserted London against heavy out-going September traffic he wondered if he would be able to declare his anger and disgust at his recent experiences and his forebodings for the future. If his cousins and their brats were in residence he would be stymied. They never took off for home until the evening, with sleeping infants stowed away in the backs of their estate cars. He must leave shortly after lunch, to be fair to the Mellishes. But he hated the thought of going on his way without at least some advice about that cheque, that frighteningly large, doubtfully earned, but certainly tempting cheque that Dr Williams had given him. He had looked at it before he finally drove away from Azalea Road. Two hundred pounds. More than twice as much as he had contracted for, considering his age and experience, or lack of it. So obviously there was an element of bribery involved. Uncle Harry must tell him how much he ought to give back. Not the whole: he had taken nearly all the night calls. He had paid for half the car hire and all the petrol, himself. But to accept the lot would be to condone the malpractice he more than suspected. A last attempt to involve him, to frame him, to prove he was already bent and would in future bend more easily.

He checked his thoughts abruptly, appalled at where

they were now leading. Again the strange duality of Dr Tom Markson linked the Overton practice with the one he had just left. Again Uncle Harry must help him. His own father, bless him, was far too trusting, far too unconcerned with misdemeanours beyond the age of thirteen to treat his son's fears as other than nightmares of a particularly lurid fantastic kind.

Then there was Lil. He admitted her attraction, strong when he was with her. But he did not really know her at all. Her history as related by herself aroused his pity, but anyone could shoot a line. Besides, she had been for the last seven years, since her aunt died, solely under the influence of that old rogue, the alcoholic James Williams. Not correct. Five or six years, since she must have stayed at her boarding school until she was seventeen or eighteen. Which raised a good many questions he had not had the opportunity or courage to ask her. Had she really no relations at all? What about her work at school? Had she no ideas for her own future, for a job of her own, a career, a profession? Had her headmistress taken no interest in her future? Had no one at the school tried to influence her?

Perhaps. He remembered her obstinate insistence upon staying with her uncle, the unfair but understandable burden laid on her by his dying wife, her own mother's sister. Poor loyal Lil. He saw her for a few moments as a romantic captive of her own integrity until the cynicism that had been growing in him since the shocking episode of Mrs Southport's accusation, rose to drown this youthful idyll.

He reached the house in Kensington a little after twelve. The door was opened to him by Uncle Harry himself.

"Good," the latter said. "Where have you parked?"

"Across the road, against the railings of the gardens. That's all right, isn't it?"

"Yes, it is. They tried to put meters there, but they took them away again. Come in."

Aunt Rachel in an overall, appeared in the hall from the kitchen at the end of it.

"We've got Emma and her friends up from the country, but Harry sent them out for a walk in the Gardens."

"I thought you sounded a bit het up on the phone," Uncle Harry said. "I thought we could have a natter in quiet if you got here in time."

"But Aunt Rachel . . . Oughtn't I to lay the table or something?"

"Certainly not," she said. "My Spanish couple are coping. I'm only doing the flowers. Go along with Harry. You won't be disturbed until the gong goes."

Settled in comfortable chairs in Sir Henry Killick's study at the front of the house, with a drink beside him and a few encouraging, skilled questions to start him off, Roy gave a rapid and reasonably full account of his locum.

"It seemed an ordinary, quite respectable practice at first," he said, summing up at the end. "It wasn't until the Southport episode that I suddenly realised there was something very wrong indeed."

"Quite," said Uncle Harry.

"It was a frame, wasn't it?"

"Clearly. The time had come to soften you up. Put the fear of God, or rather of the General Medical Council, into you. They can't have expected you to show so much resistance. I'm surprised or rather I would have been surprised they went on so quickly to make you take their licensed drug clinic."

"It really is licensed? And that nursing home, St Helen's."

"Oh yes."

"Fantastic!"

"Bureaucracy, my boy. Also the urgent need to be seen to do something useful for the hard drug addicts."

"Is it useful? Dr Williams just gives them what they want. There's no attempt to treat them. He isn't capable of it, actually. An alcoholic."

Uncle Harry nodded.

"Your attempt to treat that young man must have shaken them. I suppose the chemist warned Phillips, who employed the two thugs."

65

Roy said passionately, "Can't anything be done to stop them? It was surely an actionable assault on me!"

"Do you know the names of those two? Or where they came from?"

"No. But . . ."

"You can describe them. Not good enough. You've no proof they ever attacked you at all."

"Lill—Miss Bartlett—saw them. I bet she knows who they are."

Uncle Harry re-filled Roy's glass and then said carefully, "Ah yes, Miss Bartlett. Is she part of this racket, Roy?"

He looked keenly at his nephew as he spoke and sighed when he saw the lad's face redden. But Roy answered steadily enough, "I wish I knew. I wish I could do something for her."

"That would be very dangerous indeed," said Uncle Harry. "More for her than for you, probably."

"He's only her uncle by marriage," Roy protested.

"I'm only your uncle by marriage."

Roy laughed. Uncle Harry said, more seriously, "Isn't he the only close relation she has? He must mean a good deal to her, left an orphan, didn't you tell me, at eight years old? What was it, car or plane or what?"

"I didn't ask her," Roy answered, surprised at his own carelessness or lack of interest. He changed the subject by saying, "What bothers me most is this new practice I'm going to near Southampton. Overton, the village, is four miles out but it's almost a suburb, inshore from Fawley and the oil refinery. I'm supposed to be taking the place of a Dr Markson, who had a month to run when I was accepted as a trainee assistant. But I discovered from Lil and from the daily that the third partner I was acting locum for at Azalea Road was a Dr Markson, too. Are there two of them—Marksons, I mean? Or is this another fiddle? And how and *why?*"

Uncle Harry reached for a Sunday newspaper on the table behind his chair. It was already folded at one of the inner pages. He handed it to Roy without a word, who saw a headline which announced 'Body in the Solent'. Below there was a paragraph which read, 'At low tide yesterday morning a body was washed up near Netley. It had been in the water for some time. It proved on examination to be that of a Dr Thomas Markson. He had not been seen in the neighbourhood for three weeks. He had worked in the practice of Drs Armitage and Thompson of Overton for the first week of September, but had left after a week and was thought by them to have returned to London, where he had worked formerly."

"Yesterday!" Roy exclaimed. "Missing, then, for three weeks. *They must all have known that!*"

"They knew all right," Uncle Harry said.

Chapter 7

Lillian did not have time to look at the newspapers until after lunch that Sunday. She had to cook the meal, since Mrs Gladstone did not come on Sundays. Not that this was a very exacting task. Saturday's hot roast joint appeared cold, with a salad and a warmed-up bag of potato crisps, followed by cheese, biscuits and fruit, on this occasion, a melon.

It was not an exciting meal to prepare and with only Uncle James and herself to provide for, it took less time than usual. The old man had not moved from his study since Roy had left the house. He was well enough this morning, but that was no guarantee that he would emerge totally sober at one o'clock. Or even if he were sober, that he would be willing and able to talk during the meal.

She thought of Roy with deep regret but with her usual fatalistic lack of hope. Deep inside her she knew he was the sort of person she needed to have in her life. His robust common sense had seen him through perils with which she was only too familiar. He had changed the all too frequent melodrama into sordid reality: he had changed the fire breathing monster into a tiresome snapping dog; the treacherous serpent into a blind earthworm. Her constant dread had vanished altogether during the first three weeks of his locum. Only in the last few days had the unexpected, jolting horrors begun again. But Roy had swept through them unharmed.

To safety? She wished she could be sure of that, but there was something distinctly odd about that new practice of his and their own Dr Markson. Perhaps Uncle James . . .

At lunch Uncle James, though perfectly sober, was in the mood Lilian had foreseen, one of normal appetite and behaviour, but very few words. Bored by the long silence she said at last, "I suppose Dr Phillips was doing the visits this morning?"

"I suppose so. There will not have been many. I got Cartwright to see most of the old people on the books at least once during his locum. At least I told him to see them. I hope he did."

"He certainly did everything he was told. More, if he thought it necessary."

She spoke with some heat. Uncle James looked at her intently, seemed about to speak, but changed his mind.

"Will Dr Markson be back in time to take his morning surgery tomorrow?" she asked.

"No," Dr Williams said crossly. "No, he won't. Tomorrow or ever again—in this practice," he added.

"Do you mean he isn't coming back at all?"

"I mean exactly that."

"But surely he isn't staying . . ." She checked herself. Roy had told her the little she knew of Dr Markson's movements during the last month and he had got it from his new landlady, she supposed, or her friend in the flat at Dr Armitage's house. Not from the doctor himself.

Uncle James looked at her sharply.

"Isn't staying—where?" he demanded.

"I don't know. Just—well—staying away . . ."

It was lame, but it seemed to satisfy Dr Williams. He actually smiled at her and said, quite amiably, "Bernard told me he'd look in this afternoon to discuss times for surgeries and so on. We aren't particularly busy, plenty of people still going off on their summer holidays. So we shall take our time before we engage another—well, not locum—trainee assistant, perhaps. Or an older man looking for a partnership."

They'll never keep one, Lilian thought, not with things as they are and Uncle James getting slowly worse all the time.

"I'd prefer that," the old man went on, "an older man, I mean. I'm getting a bit rusty—don't understand half what the consultant boys mean in their reports from the hospitals. Time I retired, really."

Lilian's heart melted towards him as it always did when his real, small, frightened self peeped out for a moment, looking for help to prop him up and a breast to weep on.

"Why don't you?" she said. "We could find a cottage somewhere. Without all the anxiety and responsibility you'd be—you wouldn't be... They give you a pension, don't they? And you're already past retiring age."

"Half my average yearly income since I joined the National Health. Which I did when it started. Private practice excluded, of course. Not a very princely sum, Lil."

"There's mine to add to it. What Daddy and Mummy left. And this house belongs to you, of course."

He reached out to pat her arm.

"You've always been a good girl, Lil. Never think I'm not grateful. But I've got to carry on for a bit. Can't let old Bernard down. Always sounds as if he knew all the answers, but he doesn't, not by a long chalk. There now, I hear his car turning into the park. Tell him I'm waiting for him."

It was only after Lilian had cleared away and washed up that she took a second cup of coffee and the heavy, chatty, Sunday newspaper to her own room, settled herself in her armchair near the open window and found at the bottom of the first page the paragraph that had astonished Roy in Kensington a few hours earlier.

Dr Markson dead—drowned apparently. And three weeks ago. Neither on holiday, nor at work. But in Hampshire, in Southampton Water, drowned.

Questions rushed into her mind. Why was he there? Why had there been no search for him? Had he really been working in that practice to which Roy was now travelling? She shuddered at the proved connection. Not two Dr Marksons. One Dr Markson. *Their* Dr Markson.

He had certainly left Azalea Road the day before Roy arrived. He must have gone straight to Overton. But only for one week, it seemed. Surely the doctors at Overton would get in touch with Uncle James to discover if Markson had turned up in Azalea Road again? If so, why had Uncle James said nothing to her about the disappearance?

She went downstairs again. Dr Phillips's car was no longer in the park at the annexe so she knocked at the study door and went in holding out the folded newspaper.

"Is that what you meant when you said at lunch that Tom Markson would not be coming back?"

Dr Williams shrank down in his chair. He was paler than he had been at lunch. His hands trembled. She saw, with a sad lowering of her spirits, that he had a full glass of brandy beside him.

"You knew he was dead?"

He nodded; stretching out a hand to take the newspaper from her.

"You knew already—that he was *drowned!*"

He shook his head.

"But you knew he had disappeared? Please tell me, Uncle James! I don't understand. I'm frightened. Please tell me what's been happening! I have a right to know. How can I stay here, if I'm never told what's going on? Never . . ."

She was crying now, both hands up to her face to hide her tears, her sobs tearing at her.

"I can't tell you anything," Uncle James said, thickly. "Go away, girl. Go away, you damned, smarmy, sneaking, hysterical, bloody little fool! Get out of my sight! Didn't you hear? Get out . . ."

He was struggling to his feet, incoherent and breathless with half-drunken rage and fear. Lilian turned and ran from the room.

Roy had been right, she thought. This was no longer a home, a place where as a child she had found the security and love so suddenly taken from her at her parents' death. No longer a home, but a strange, foreign place hidden all these years under the guise of a home, but now revealed in all its bewildering strangeness and menace. Even perhaps a prison, she decided, shuddering as she remembered Dr Phillips's warning to her when he had called her back into the annexe after she had left it with Roy the night before, or rather one o'clock that same day.

"Keep to your own job, Lilian," he had told her in the

71

icy, hectoring tone she always feared. "Help your uncle, look after the records, but keep your inquisitive little nose out of the practice itself. Don't try to interfere with the patients, just introduce them to us at their appointments."

"If you aren't satisfied, Dr Phillips, I will ask Uncle James to find an outside receptionist," she had answered, daring to speak so because she had been able to help Roy, or hoped she had done so.

"I strongly advise you not to bother your uncle at all with your tantrums," he had said. "And not to come down to the surgery indecently dressed. Some of our patients are capable of misunderstanding your intention and taking advantage of it."

His face as he said this wore such a bleakly evil expression that she had not dared to speak again. But this cold bullying mattered less than the resolve beneath it, which was to keep her in the service of the practice because she already knew too much about it and because Dr Phillips needed her to keep Dr Williams as its nominal head.

So perhaps a prison, she thought, as she sat in her room recovering from Uncle James's violent dismissal. And yet, in this day and age, how could that be? Was it not all in her own head, not in any kind of reality? She thought of Roy, but there was little comfort in the exercise. He had gone and even if he had carried the mystery of Tom Markson with him to his new job, he must surely find it solved for him in the coroner's court now that the poor lad's body had been found and the police could ask their questions and demand the answers.

Perhaps she should have told Roy more about Tom, but there had seemed to be no occasion to do so. He had been with them as a trainee assistant for two years and junior partner for six months before he left on what she understood was a holiday, a perfectly normal holiday, though longer than the usual fortnight. The next day Roy came as locum.

Tom Markson was a Eurasian: English father, Indian

mother, both living in India where the father was in business. Tom had come to England to train as a doctor. He was quiet, polite, well educated, with adequate·hospital experience after qualifying. He wanted to get further insight into ordinary general practice before going back to India to follow his profession there.

Until the episode with Mrs Southport, so exactly like the recent one that Roy had suffered. Tom Markson had made no immediate criticism of the practice at Azalea Road, no comment of any kind, certainly not to herself. He had continued his work, quietly and efficiently.

But not happily. That at least she had noticed and remembered it now with a sense of guilt. Yet what could she have done? Though always polite he had never been friendly. He had never shown any inclination to discuss the Southport affair with her. Ought she to have attempted to speak of it to him? Perhaps if he had reacted as Roy had, with anger and disgust and instant suspicion, she would have been ready to help. But at the time, she was ashamed now to realise, she had admitted the possibility of some truth in the accusation. Simply because Tom Markson was a foreigner and a non-European.

Lilian spent the next two days in a state of apathy, deepening into profound depression and unmoving boredom. But on Wednesday she had a letter from Roy that immediately restored her usually sanguine outlook. He was settling into the new practice, which was brisk and interesting, though the two principals were much shaken by the apparently motiveless suicide of Dr Markson. The inquest had been postponed to allow the victim's father to travel from India to identify the body. It appeared that he had been at Overton for only a week before he left. They had not told Roy this when they engaged him because they hoped Tom would turn up again to complete his month. Markson had told them almost at once that the practice was not suitable for him, not what he expected. But he had not told them why this was, nor how he had come to such a rapid decision.

Roy ended his letter with an invitation.

'I am coming up to London,' he wrote, 'on Saturday afternoon to collect a few things I left with my uncle and aunt who live in Kensington. I have to get back to Overton that night but can you come along to dinner about seven for seven-thirty? I'd like you to meet them. I want to tell you more of my news and hear yours. Above all to see you, darling Lil.'

It was a very splendid answer to more than unbelieving prayer, Lilian decided, because she had forced herself to think she would never see or hear of Roy again. She wrote a very short answer of acceptance, put a fivepenny stamp on the envelope and took it out at once to the post.

The Killicks' house in Kensington was all Lilian expected. She had looked up the name in the telephone directory, finding Sir Henry Killick Q.C. at the address to which she had been bidden. In a fit of snobbery she wrote another note, very formal, to Lady Killick explaining Roy's invitation for Saturday and accepting it with pleasure, hoping it was authentic. She then tore this up, threw the pieces in her waste-paper basket, collected them out of it again and took them to the kitchen boiler stove to burn. But she did not throw away Roy's letter and during the next three days read it again and again. On her shopping expedition on Wednesday she visited the local Public Library to look up Sir Henry Killick in *Who's Who*. She found he was sixty-one, had had a rapid and successful rise to his present eminence and had achieved fame in several notorious criminal cases of the last twenty years. If he was Roy's uncle he must be related to Mrs Cartwright. A familiar relationship.

Armed with these facts, hoping she had done right in accepting Roy's invitation direct, hoping the evening would not prove embarrassing, Lilian travelled by train and Tube and found herself a correct five minutes late, climbing four steps to a porticoed Victorian front door in a pleasant square whose central garden was neatly maintained with late dahlias and early chrysanthemums glowing in the orange late September dying sun.

The door was opened by Roy, eager, smiling, both hands

74

out to pull her into his arms. It was a friendly hug. He dropped a kiss on the side of her neck, careful to avoid ruining her make-up. Her heart warmed to his consideration. She was thrilled and uplifted by the sense of easy understanding between them. At Azalea Road she had been willing to put it down to the poverty of her outside friendships; half a dozen school friends, scattered now over the British Isles; a slightly larger number of local acquaintences, all women, who were connected with her uncle and aunt in former times. Their children had come to parties at Azalea Road while Aunt Emily was alive and she had gone to theirs, but when she was alone with Uncle James the parties had stopped—the friendships had withered.

"Let me take your coat," Roy was saying. "You look marvellous. Fantastic."

She smiled at him. The dress was in its third year. She had been chasing the hem up her thighs each season, but recently at a slower rate. It was a very simple dress, sleeveless, high at the neck, made of an ivory-coloured heavy cotton material, avoiding lurex and any other form of glitter. But at the neck she wore a diamond and ruby brooch that had belonged to her mother, who had it from *her* mother, who had worn it in late Victorian times, one of many tokens of her husband's growing prosperity.

"Come and meet the uncle and aunt," Roy said, taking her hand.

The large drawing room was as predictable as the front of the house, Lilian thought. The Killicks were friendly and kind, Roy's Aunt Rachel in particular. She settled the very shy girl on a sofa, brought her a glass of sherry and sat down beside her.

"I'm very lucky," she said. "I have a pair of first-class Spanish girls, aunt and young niece. They don't seem to mind how long they work or when. So if we have people to dinner like this they just stay on and seem to think it's fun for them, too, bless their Mediterranean hearts."

"They don't live in, then?" Lilian asked. Not a very clever question but she felt she must say something.

"No. The older one has a husband working at one of the big hospitals hereabouts. They left their two children in Spain with the parents of the niece."

Domestic conversation went on happily. Lilian found herself describing her own arrangements at 38 Azalea Road, with a full account of the invaluable Mrs Gladstone.

"She's been working for my uncle for years," she said. "Certainly she was there when I was eight because she used to take me to school when I first went to live there."

"Roy told me about your parents," Aunt Rachel said sympathetically. "You've had a great deal of responsibility for someone so young."

"Not at first," Lilian said. "There was a living-in cook and of course my Aunt Emily. Then I was at boarding school. It's only been since I left..."

She stopped herself. To go on would mean complaining or worse still confiding the actual, present build-up of suspicion and worry and shame.

Lady Killick did not press her. In fact she gave a signal, that Lilian noticed with amusement, to her husband, who came across the room with a third man. The girl had not noticed his arrival; she wondered how many more people there would be at this dinner party.

"Miss Bartlett, this is Commander Hull."

The tall, grey-haired, broad-shouldered new arrival in the dark grey suit shook hands with Lilian while Sir Henry went on speaking. "Miss Bartlett keeps house for her doctor uncle," he explained, "who runs the practice where Roy has just finished his first plunge into real medicine."

Roy, who had joined them, turned a deep red. Lilian paled a little. Had Roy's Uncle Harry placed a slight emphasis on the word 'real'? Had Commander Hull's friendly glance sharpened quickly for a second before relaxing into amusement?

Lady Killick moved towards the door of the room.

"I'll just see if those two realise we're all present and correct?" she said.

"Time to show Lil your prize dahlias?" Roy asked.

"Not to do them justice," the barrister answered. "No. Here's Rachel back with good news. After dinner, Roy."

The dinner was delicious, the Killicks were dears, Lilian decided, staring dreamy-eyed at a variety of bright dahlia heads in the garden, Roy's arm round her waist, her own hand on his shoulder. The sailor man had been very silent, but who cared? Uncle Harry told funny legal stories, Roy described his very nice present digs, the slightly comic partner in the new practice, the very knowledgeable principal, the new patients, the new problems.

"Mixed bag," he told them. "Lots of temporaries off the ships, all colours, shapes and sizes."

"Crews, you mean?" asked Commander Hull making one of his infrequent remarks.

"Some. Not all, by any means. Tourists, American chiefly. The Europeans, I imagine, make the short crossing to Dover by preference, if they don't fly. And students at the University, of course."

There was a little serious conversation on the problems of newcomers from abroad, but Uncle Harry did not allow it to become solemn. As he moved back into the house Roy kept Lilian behind the others. The light had nearly faded, it was growing cold.

"This is a lovely house and lovely people," she said, happily. "You are very lucky to have them, Roy. You know that, I hope."

He kissed her suddenly, long and hard, then turned her away from the dahlias and took her back indoors.

Knowing that he had to drive to Overton that night, Lilian decided she must now go home and said so.

"I'll drive you," Roy said. "It's not much out of my way."

"It's miles out. Besides, I came on a train most of the way. You can take me to Victoria if you like."

"London Bridge."

"All right."

Just before they got there Lilian said, "When was

Commander Hull in the Navy? The war, I suppose. He's retired now, isn't he?"

Roy laughed.

"Neither the Navy nor retired, love. A very very high-up chap at Scotland Yard."

Lilian was speechless.

"Never heard of the rank? Don't you ever read thrillers? Uncle Harry knows a lot of cops. He made his name defending villains, as they call them still. To look at Hull you wouldn't think he'd kill a fly. But he wouldn't be where he is if he hadn't been pretty ruthless on the way up."

Lilian made no answer. All the way home she felt her heart shrivelling, her newborn hopes blackening, as the Killick dahlias would blacken and shrivel when the first frosts came.

Chapter 8

By the time she reached home Lilian's innate good sense had brought her out of the gloom into which Roy's final announcement had cast her. Naturally with his uncle so high in the legal profession he had told him about the strange goings-on at Azalea Road. Naturally Sir Henry had taken the opportunity of Roy's visit and invitation to the girl friend to inspect her. Perhaps he had even suggested meeting her himself, but got Roy to invite her so that, if she were part of the questionable side of the practice, she would not be warned and refuse.

She had not been warned. She had been treated with unusual consideration and lulled into such complete confidence that she had told Lady Killick far more about her family and herself than she had ever done before to a complete stranger. Well, it must all have sounded perfectly innocent; a sad real life tale of an orphaned childhood saved from disaster by kind relations. She had suggested that Uncle James was getting old and was not in good health. She had scarcely mentioned Bernard Phillips. So perhaps she herself had been cleared as far as the Killicks were concerned.

But was Roy really being used by his uncle or had he organised this plan to scrutinise her, or was she imagining far more than was probable? She understood quite clearly that her whole revulsion of feeling had been caused by Roy's remark about Commander Hull of Scotland Yard.

So what? Would Roy have blurted it out, have found her mistake highly amusing, if the cop had been there on business, to sum her up, instead of merely as an old friend of the Killicks? Of course not. Again she absolved Roy of complicity. Any guile, any mistrust, belonged solely to the lawyer, who couldn't help exercising his professional ability even out of hours, she decided bitterly.

The hall of 38 Azalea Road was in darkness but there

was a light on in Uncle James's study. Lilian went in. Uncle James was writing at his desk. Dr Phillips was sitting near the electric fire, reading an evening newspaper. Both men looked up as she appeared. She shut the door carefully behind her. The room was very hot as usual, but there were no glasses or bottles in sight; this was very far from usual.

"You're late in," Uncle James said.

"Am I?" She looked at her watch. "It's only just after ten."

She had told her uncle quite truthfully that she was meeting a friend for dinner in Kensington.

"Young Cartwright liking his new job?" Dr Phillips asked, with a glance at his partner.

"Yes." There was no point in denying she had been with Roy. They were both looking at her, they both knew. How?

She turned to leave them. But Dr Phillips went on, "How did you find his posh relations?"

She remembered burning her draft letter to Lady Killick. But she had kept Roy's. In the desk in her room. She turned back again, ignoring Phillips, appealing to her uncle.

"Since when have you been searching my private writing desk?" she asked. "Or does that job fall to Dr Phillips?"

Neither of them answered at once, so she said goodnight as calmly as she could and left the room. But as she shut the door behind her slowly she heard Uncle James say, "You crazy idiot, Bernard. Will you never learn that the girl has brains!"

"Sharp as a new hypodermic needle, eh?" Dr Phillips sneered, but there was frustrated anger in his voice.

Lilian had finished closing the door so she did not hear this remark nor her uncle's broken reply.

"Don't underrate her. That's all I mean. I wish now I'd got her out of here years ago. But when Emily died..." He broke off, looking round for the bottle that Bernard had forbidden earlier. "Can't we..."

"Not yet," Dr Phillips said. "Have you finished that fairy tale they call..."

"A deposition," Dr Williams said. "For you to put in at the inquest. With my certificate of unfitness to attend by reason of chronic bronchitis with emphysema. Signed E. Waters, MB BS."

"Faithful little runt," Dr Phillips said, looking at the signature on the certificate. "Always takes the dictation like a lamb."

"It happens to be true. Of course he's faithful. Didn't I cover up for him and save the child's life when he was hooked on anaesthetics and nearly passed out taking my young patient with him? That taught him a lesson he's never forgotten. He's been on the level for years. He'll not go off it again. And he's still grateful."

Dr Phillips was silent, withdrawn. He did not seem to have heard his partner's rather wandering explanation. But after a few minutes he got up, stretching and yawning.

"Bed," he said, "and I hope to God there are no night calls for you."

"For you, Bernard. I could hardly take them after that certificate, could I? I know I'll have to totter into the surgery tomorrow morning, but not a step further."

"Damn you!" Dr Phillips said from the door. "Bloody slippery old twister! I don't know why I go on propping you up as I do."

"Because if you didn't you'd fall flat on your own face," Dr Williams answered, grinning. But when Phillips had gone he collapsed at his desk, his arms in front of him, his face between them.

Lilian found him like this when she went down again to the study, having heard Dr Phillips's car drive away. There was still no bottle visible, no empty glasses, so Uncle James must be genuinely ill and no wonder, with the day's news about Tom Markson and the way she had capped it with her visit to Kensington to Roy's distinguished and potentially dangerous uncle.

She helped Dr Williams to his bedroom, then went to her own, too tired after all the varied excitements and pleasures and pains of that day to worry about the future.

The first half of the next week passed quietly for Lilian. She realised by Wednesday that Roy must have been

81

doing a very full day's work in the practice while he was with them. September had not been like July, with more than half the patients away on holiday. In September most of them were back, with colds and upset tummies acquired abroad or at the native resorts; or simply with post-holiday depression at the thought of another year's work to face and an empty bank balance as well.

Uncle James, however, seemed to have accepted the need for serious effort. Dr Phillips, too, avoided open revolt or even complaint, rather to Lilian's surprise, since it was she who had to book visits and appointments for him. Many of the calls were for Roy and many were the regrets that he had left Azalea Road and was not to be found anywhere in London.

Letters, too, came for Roy and since they were very likely to contain requests for more medicine, she opened them all to find out. She was very nearly always right and able to pass the letters on to Dr Williams. One or two were from friends and these she forwarded with a slip enclosed to explain what she had done and why. One was from the addict case who had caused so much trouble at Roy's last late-night surgery. The boy's experience, drastic indeed, had shaken him in a most salutory manner. He had been taken in charge as a drunk, he wrote, but diagnosed correctly by a police doctor. When partially recovered he had asked, in a panic, for his parents and been taken home by his father. The chemist had confirmed his legitimate prescription. He had gone back into hospital for treatment aimed at curing the addiction. He wanted to thank Roy and would be glad to see him again some time.

Lilian put her duplicated note with this letter when she forwarded it. No wonder Dr Phillips had been badly scared. No wonder he had attempted to silence Roy by violent means that had failed and by baseless threats that had no greater success. That had, in fact, only stirred him to discover more about this whole dubious business.

For Lilian had changed her mind considerably over the last few days. Roy's anger was justified. If he was firmly in pursuit of the truth of these shady actions, then Sir Henry was exactly the right sort of person to help him.

Probably, though she still winced at her memory of him, the non-naval Commander, Mr Top-Brass-Detective Hull, as well.

On Thursday Lilian saw that Uncle James was feeling the strain of his heroic effort in the practice and taking to the bottle again in a big way so as to fortify its continuance. She knew it would have the opposite effect as always, and this led her to consider, once more, why such a formerly charming, gifted man had declined so pitifully. Aunt Emily had never tried to hide his faults or explain them away by lies. She had generously put his drunkeness down more to grief at the loss of his first wife than to innate, incurable weakness. For the first time Lilian began to wonder why this grief had been so inconsolable, so intense, why it had found such distrastrous expression, why Aunt Emily's goodness and love had never been able to relieve it.

From these insistent questions the girl passed on to considering where she might find an answer or rather from whom. Obviously from someone who had known this shadowy, much-loved forerunner of her own dear aunt. But she knew nothing about the woman, except that she had died in the late twenties. There had been no children. No relation of hers had ever, as far as she knew, been in touch with Uncle James. Perhaps there was no contemporary relation still living. Her uncle was sixty-eight, his first wife had been about his age, it was quite likely any brother or sister had died by now.

So who to ask? An early patient, of course, if any such still existed. With luck still living in the neighbourhood. For the practice had not moved, however much its surroundings had altered.

From this point Lilian settled down to a reasonable, well-thought-out research into the records. In the old days there had been a very flourishing private practice and a limited National Insurance list of working people from two big and several small factories in the neighbourhood. Also a large number of women in secretarial jobs or behind the counter jobs, also insured nationally. None of these was likely to help her. But the private patients, the small shopkeepers, the school teachers, the bank clerks and high up the scale the business men, managers, professionals of all kinds, surely they or their wives might help. Young Dr Williams and his wife must surely have entertained normally and been asked to parties in their turn. Was it quite impossible to discover any of them? Was there no one to ask? It was very long ago. To Lilian it seemed to have happened in pre-history. Ten years or so before the War. The Second War Uncle James always called it. Any patient from that First War would be, unless a child at the time, over seventy today. Where then could he or she be found?

It was not going to be an easy matter to discover. Lilian knew that a very large number of the former private patients had joined the National Health Service as soon as it was formed. So any medical records Dr Williams had kept for them had been put into the new folders. To search through the whole two thousand or more of these filed records, perhaps not accurately dated, would take weeks, perhaps months. For Dr Williams's lot, alone, not counting the other two thousand or so belonging to Dr Phillips.

Lilian was very conscious of the need for secrecy in her search. Uncle James expected her to keep the records in their cabinets in correct alphabetical order, in order to produce them quickly during surgery hours. The cards of the remaining private patients, shrinking in number all the time now, were still kept in their old boxes in Dr Williams's study.

When her uncle was safely in the annexe and Mrs Gladstone occupied in the kitchen with lunch, Lilian found an opportunity to inspect these records, passing over the occasional new white cards to concentrate on the yellowing ones with remarks in fading ink written with a broad nib before her uncle had taken to a ball-point pen.

But she very soon gave this up for an easier line of research. She noticed on one card a statement in brackets. (Account still unsettled ?send reminder ?to Johnson.) The patient had been seen on this occasion, treatment had been prescribed, a date had been given for a further

84

consultation. But there the record ended. Had the patient flitted? Had the reminder or Mr Johnson, whoever he might be—presumably some kind of collector of unpaid fees—frightened him off? The last date was in March 1930. Just the sort of patient she was looking for, but presumably lost for ever on account of that unpaid bill. Or had he paid it before turning down Uncle James, who insisted so uncharitably on dunning a poor invalid? Though the patient's address in the wealthier part of the neighbourhood did not suggest he had been on the bread line.

Her curiosity over this patient showed Lilian a far quicker way of discovering what she wanted than ploughing through records in the study. In her own little office she held the private patients' account cards in a filing cabinet that went back to the very beginning of the practice. The dates on these cards must be accurate. The information they gave was far more to her purpose than the medical records and gave her none of the uneasiness she had felt in reading such highly confidential detail.

The patient who had been so reluctant to pay his medical adviser had settled his bill in the end, she was amused to find. But not until Uncle James had appealed for help to the solicitors of his medical insurance society. Her further researches were equally productive. She was able to cross check those patients whose private accounts stopped because they had joined the Health Service and to ignore all those whose accounts began after 1930. She was left with a few names, a very few, mostly women who were faithful to their old doctor and still appealed to him for help as private patients more than forty years later. A slightly larger number seemed to have left the practice in 1931. On looking up both groups in the telephone directory Lilian was able to check the first lot, several with new addresses and also to discover two of the latter who still lived where they had done in 1931.

Not all of the 'originals' as she now thought of them were in the directory. Probably they were dead or had left London altogether. She decided to eliminate them by careful and seemingly casual questions at shops in the neighbourhood of their former dwellings. At the same time she started a discreet line of inquiry by calling the small number of those who did appear in the telephone list.

"This is Dr Williams's secretary," she would begin. "May I speak to——please?"

The answer in most cases was given by the person she sought.

"I am re-arranging the doctor's record," she would continue. "It is a considerable time since you consulted Dr Williams. May I assume you do not still consider yourself a patient of his?"

The answer was usually an unqualified agreement with that polite assumption, no explanation and the end of the call. But in three cases, two of which were not given in person by the patient, but by some unspecified relation, attendant or friend, there was anger, scarcely hidden.

"I am surprised Dr Williams has the face to ask such a question. Secretary, are you? Then of course you don't know," one said. And the other, "He hasn't told you? My aunt forbid him ever to call at her house again? Certainly she changed her doctor directly after the inquest."

The third, in a quavering voice of extreme old age, told her that Mr Longhorn was as well as could be expected at his present age of ninety-six, and would prefer not to be taken off Dr Williams's list. He might need him yet, if only to look at his congratulation from the Queen when he reached his hundredth birthday. A high cackle of ancient laughter ended the call.

At the beginning of the next week Lilian found herself left with a very meagre set of conclusions, though she was able to tear up and dispose of a good many useless cards. She did this without reference to Dr Williams. His medical records, such as they were, had not been altered. Obviously no one could be interested now in the fees paid by patients who had attended in the twenties and left the practice by 1931. Except those three with a grievance or a judgment or whatever it was. Something about Dr Williams had upset them in that year. And the first Mrs Williams had died in 1930. Any connection? If so, what? But who would tell her? Certainly not those three.

She approached the subject in a roundabout way with Mrs Gladstone. The latter knew all there was to know about her uncle's failing. Indeed, without Mrs Gladstone, she would not have been able to go on living at Azalea Road.

"Gladdy," she said, using the name she had invented when she was a child and used ever since. "Uncle James has been much better ever since Roy left, in spite of having to take all his own surgeries."

"Pleased to hear it," Mrs Gladstone answered. "Honest work never did no harm to nobody."

After a suitable pause, Lilian said, "Was he always like this? Aunt Emily said it started after his first wife died, but he may just have told her that."

"Very likely," Mrs Gladstone agreed. "It takes 'em that way. Lie like children."

"So there's no way I can find out?"

"Is it so important to you to know, Miss Lilian? Stands to reason I can't tell you, seeing I've only been coming here the last six years."

"Oh but Gladdy, surely it was you who took me for walks when I was eight, if Aunt Emily couldn't? That's why I call you Gladdy."

"I wasn't working 'ere then. Not till very much later."

Lilian changed the subject. It would not do to make Mrs Gladstone suspicious. She was devoted to both the doctors, Bernard Phillips in particular. She was both indulgent and compassionate over Uncle James's 'failing' as she called it. If she thought Lilian had any ulterior motive in her questions that might endanger the practice or either of the partners she was quite capable of telling them about those activities. Not that she knew about the records and the telephone calls. Or did she?

While Lilian did nothing for the next few days, letting matters rest outwardly but allowing her thoughts free range, she had a letter from Roy. It was lively and amusing about his new work, uninhibited about his growing regard for herself. At the very end, in a postcript, he wrote, 'The inquest on Tom Markson was held today. Identification only. Medical evidence postponed, because not complete. Adjourned indefinitely.'

Chapter 9

With this piece of information to relay to Mrs Gladstone Lilian began a fresh attempt to discover more about the shady side of her uncle's practice.

"They don't seem to be getting on very fast with the inquest on poor Dr Markson," she began.

"Can't say I've taken all that interest," Mrs Gladstone answered.

"Well I have," Lilian said, briskly. "They waited to get his father all the way here from India to identify the body. Uncle James said it would be difficult after three weeks in the water."

"You always did like to harp on the horrors, Miss Lilian. I'd rather not listen to that sort of talk."

"But it matters, Gladdy. It's worrying Uncle James terribly, which makes him drink more and that makes Dr Phillips furious. What I don't understand is why those doctors at Overton didn't identify Dr Markson and why our two weren't asked to do so. Dr Phillips wasn't asked to identify, only to give an account of Tom's work here and a statement from Uncle James. And then, after all, this wasn't asked for because the medical report wasn't ready. The whole thing was adjourned."

"I don't see what it has to do with us," Mrs Gladstone persisted.

"I do. I want to know what Tom was doing near Southampton when he was supposed to be on holiday. And why he went straight from here to Overton and stayed a week working for them and then disappeared. Was all this his own doing? Did he fix that other job without telling Uncle James? Did he not tell them at Overton that he had been working here?"

"If he was planning his suicide it would seem natural

to me he'd do all of that," Mrs Gladstone answered, calmly.

"Yes, I suppose so. But we don't know yet it *was* suicide, do we? The inquest being adjourned seems to suggest it may not have been."

"You're thinking of poor young Dr Smith that took an overdose, are you?"

"I am indeed, Gladdy. But that was before Aunt Emily died, when I was too young to know what really happened. Tell me."

"I'm not sure I ever knew rightly. Only he began to take the drugs himself and give himself an overdose, like I said. Accidental death, the coroner give it."

"How did he get hold of drugs? It was long before the clinic was set up."

"There wasn't such a need for it. But Dr Williams treated several for addiction even in them days. Had sympathy for those that couldn't control theirselves. Drink with him, poor gentleman. Injections with them others. There wasn't the same range of pills they has today."

"Perhaps Dr Markson was an addict too and that made him take an overdose. Not that I ever saw any sign of it with him."

"Nor I. And how'd he get in the water, then? No, Miss Lilian, not likely. Dr Williams or Dr Phillips would have known of it and helped him."

"Uncle James would have. I'm not so sure about Dr Phillips."

Mrs Gladstone was up in arms at once, but half laughing at the same time.

"I won't have you speak against Dr Phillips, Miss Lilian, as you well know. He did more for me than most doctors would have at the time."

Lilian thought the moment was right to pursue this subject as she had often wanted to do.

"How was that?" she asked. "You often say it, but you've never told me how he was so good to you."

"It was when my hubby died. I just couldn't face another and the youngest turned seven as it was. He took me in St Helen's."

"For an abortion, you mean?"

Mrs Gladstone winced at the word.

"It's all very well for you these days," she said. "Think nothing of it—no disgrace, neither. But it were illegal, then. He risked being struck off, notwithstanding I had a sustificate I was liable to a nervous breakdown, unless."

"They did that in those days as well? Did it always work?"

"I know nothing of that. But Dr Phillips did all that was necessary and charged very moderate for it, too, considering."

Lilian was revolted. She could not help exclaiming, "He actually made you pay a fee?"

"Not to him. It was St Helen's expenses. Quite right, too."

Lilian was silenced. Quite wrong, she thought. The shark. Not his fee! When the so-called nursing home, the illegal abortion shop, was his, run and maintained by him. Big profits in those days. You stressed the immense risks, you charged the frightened, desperate women accordingly.

"My uncle never charged fees to his own household," she said, smoothly, transferring her anger because she did not want to stop Mrs Gladstone in her present expansive mood. "He has never charged anything to people like health visitors or nurses."

"They'd mostly be on the old National Insurance," Mrs Gladstone said.

"Not nurses belonging to private associations," Lilian answered. "Or retired ones."

This gave her an idea she had not yet considered.

"I know he used to see several retired patients at one time," she said. "Wasn't there a Miss Tims? She hasn't been up for years."

"She's still about," Mrs Gladstone said. "State registered nurse, she was. Did part-time at St Helen's from time to time. Keeps well. I often speak to her. She always asks after the doctor."

"Meaning Uncle James? Not Dr Phillips?"

"Get along with you!" Mrs Gladstone said, laughing heartily. "You can't get a rise out of me, Miss Lilian and you know it!"

Lilian went away in a more cheerful frame of mind. Perhaps she had allowed herself to suspect her uncle's partner of evil deeds when all the time both he and Uncle James had acted no worse than many of their contemporaries. If Dr Phillips had been caught and convicted and punished for procuring abortions while they were illegal, he would have been condemned as well in his profession, not for moral turpitude so much as for being found guilty of criminal behaviour.

All the same their motives, at least Dr Phillips's motive, had been greed of gain. That was certain. She wondered how much Phillips had extracted from poor old Gladdy, left with her big family to support and terrified of having yet another mouth to feed.

Miss Tims, retired nurse, did not appear in the private accounts files because she paid no fees. She did, however, have a card among those of the private patients's records, quite an interesting card, for Dr Williams gave dates of his visits to her and they were regular monthly ones, going back over the years. Just a date in the first week of every month for fifteen years, four columns of dates on each side of every card. Before 1955 there had been only occasional entries with beside them I.S.Q., which she knew meant 'In status quo' for 'In status quo ante' or 'the same as before.'

Lilian put away Miss Tims's records. Uncle James had not yet been to see the old nurse that month and the first week was over, well over. In the first week Roy had gone away after the strange happenings in the surgery. Since then Tom Markson's body had been found. Had her uncle forgotten the old girl in the middle of these excitements? It would surely be quite in order for her to call and make excuses for him. Surely quite in order.

Miss Tims opened her door with an eager look on her face. She lived some distance from Azalea Road, on one of the early Council estates, where she had a ground-floor flat converted from the original two storey house. When she saw Lilian her face changed.

"The room's taken," she said, pulling in her lips. "And I only let the one. There's no board up. I took it down yesterday. Didn't you see?"

"But I don't want a room," Lilian said, smiling. "I'm Dr Williams's niece. My name's Lilian Bartlett. May I come in?"

Miss Tims was all smiles as she stood aside for Lilian to enter.

"I do apologise, Miss . . ."

"Bartlett."

"Miss Bartlett. You see I help out my pension letting a room. The Council is good to me in that respect. But just the one and out all day. Provides her own food."

"I see."

"The room on your left, Miss Bartlett. It gets about of course that I live alone except for my lodger. So they think I'll take more. But I couldn't do with more than one."

Lilian found herself in a pleasant small sitting room rather over-crowded with chairs and tables and photographs. But there was a modern electric fire in the grate and a large television outfit occupying the whole of one corner of the room. Quite a prosperous scene, if old-fashioned, Lilian decided. She took the chair she was offered. Miss Tims also sat, silent now but clearly expectant.

"I know my uncle comes to see you every month," Lilian began. "So as I was passing I thought I would call as well."

"Yes?" said Miss Tims, on a questioning note.

"You look very well. I think I remember your face. When Mrs Williams, the second Mrs Williams, my Aunt Emily, was alive. I came to live with them . . ."

"I remember you very well now," said Miss Tims. "I was not expecting to see you and the way they keep bothering me for rooms, students and that . . ."

"Why should you remember me at all," Lilian said,

smiling. "Apart from the letting rooms bother, you quite enjoy your retirement, do you?"

Miss Tims shook her head impatiently.

"I'd be bored without the letting. If I hadn't got the tele I'd be round the bend in no time."

"I'm sure you wouldn't," Lilian said. Openings were proving more difficult to find than she expected. "I'm sure you've always been interested in people and their troubles."

It was forced, not very sincere, because Miss Tims had, on the whole, a hard face, intelligent, alert, but definitely unfeeling.

She plunged on, since she got no response.

"Isn't it rather a satisfaction to know you have all those years of helping people behind you?"

"I know I'm glad they *are* behind me."

"You must have been qualified as a nurse about the same time as Dr Williams was as a doctor. Were you here when he took on the practice?"

"Oh yes. I was here. I was here the whole of my time."

"Then you will have known his first wife?"

A slow change came over Miss Tims's face. It did not exactly soften, it blurred. Where before she had seemed expectant, now she gave an impression of retreat, of going into hiding, while using a peephole to keep in contact with the enemy. Why does she think I'm an enemy, Lilian asked herself, beginning in her turn to be afraid. She pulled herself together.

"I don't suppose you got to know her well," she said, boldly. "She died fairly soon after they came here, didn't she?"

Miss Tims did not answer this directly. She got up and walked to the window, looked out at Lilian's small car and walked back.

"You want me to tell you how she died, don't you?" she said, standing before Lilian, between her and the door. "Did he send you?"

"Who? Uncle James?"

"Yes. The old soak. He's been talking at last, has he? I wondered when it would happen. He's retiring, is he?"

Lilian stared. But she knew her mission had failed. She had gained nothing from it but more suspicion, consequently more uneasiness.

"I don't really know what you mean," she said. "But I can't listen to that sort of talk about Dr Williams. And as far as I know he hasn't the slightest intention of retiring at present. Certainly he didn't send me to you. I came, because..."

"Because what?"

"Because you know he always calls and this month he hasn't. I thought you might be hurt. Is that it?"

"Yes, if you must know. It is."

Her face gave up childish sulks for equally childish cunning.

"But you haven't brought it? Have you?"

"Brought what?"

"The usual. You haven't brought it?"

"Now I *really* don't know what you mean. What *is* the usual? Money?"

Miss Tims drew herself up, the offended dignity of a dowager.

"Dr Williams has always been very good to me," she said.

Lilian went away. More corruption, bribery or blackmail, it came to much the same thing, she decided. And she was up against the barrier again. Impossible to go to Uncle James and say, "I paid a visit to Miss Tims today. I thought I might get her to tell me about your first wife's death and why you gave up surgery afterwards when you were doing quite a lot of private operations before. Why are you giving her a monthly present of money? Kindness of heart or blackmail? What does she know about you that must be hidden?"

No. None of that could be said. Lilian was appalled when she went over the whole business in her mind that evening, after she had taken the coffee tray away to the kitchen and Uncle James had gone into his study to write some letters. Or so he had told her.

There seemed to be no end, she thought, to the dubious

ways of the two men whose work provided her with her living, her protection, her home. You peeled the onion, layer on layer, finding the rotten core appear in more and more places. She was coming reluctantly to decide she must give up her trust if she was not to be destroyed by it.

But even this would not be easy. Dr Phillips was ruthless; she had proved that over the years. He was now becoming reckless. If Roy had not defended himself so well or had been ready to ask for redress in the courts a great deal of curious fact about Dr Phillips would inevitably have been made public. The self-assured bully would not have made such a mistaken judgment in his second attack on Roy. Even if he had indeed been led into the earlier Mrs Southport incident, by his success in a similar attempt on Tom Markson. She remembered how Tom had told her he had been misunderstood, treated unjustly, grossly libelled. But he had not stood up for himself as Roy had done. Perhaps Tom, realizing his inner cowardice had so come to despise himself that he had taken his own life. No, that was not at all the Tom she had known. Cowardice had not brought about his death.

Though Lilian had no intention of telling her uncle that she had been to see Miss Tims, still less of asking him about his own relations with the retired nurse, she did at the end of that week find herself describing her visit.

Uncle James began it. He suddenly put down the newspaper he was reading at breakfast and asked in an irritated voice, "What possessed you to go bothering old Nurse Tims? I saw her yesterday."

"She sent a note asking for a visit, didn't she?"

"You haven't answered my question."

"Why I went to see her? I thought as she was such an old patient—I mean had been on your books for so long—she's not so very old in years—only seventyish, I think..."

"How did you know that...? That she'd been a patient for so long?"

"Gladdy told me. We were saying not many of the really old ones could manage to get up to the surgery... I think it was the morning Mr Cleat tottered in. He must be nearly a hundred, isn't he?"

"Don't change the subject. We were discussing your visit to Nurse Tims."

"What about it? She told you I'd been to see her. There was nothing much to tell about it or did she make up a story?"

Dr Williams glared at her. It was his only response to frustration; Lilian had long ago ceased to be alarmed by it. But when he mumbled something about keeping the medical records to himself and only allowing her access to the accounts, she said in exasperation, "Why not engage a proper secretary, Uncle James? One who is only interested in the weekly pay packet, not in the practice or the patients. I'm sure I could find an outside job, even without any sort of diploma. I did get four A levels."

"Don't be ridiculous," Uncle James said, but he dropped the subject of Miss Tims and never referred to her again.

Chapter 10

Lilian found no consolation in the days that followed. Her uncle recovered a little from his latest bout of drinking and managed to present a sober appearance in the consulting room. But this was his usual pattern; it held no comfort for her, nor any promise for the future. Mrs Gladstone was distant, very restrained in her speech, not unkind but far from her ordinary affectionate self. Lilian suspected that she had been questioned by Uncle James and perhaps had a strip torn off for talking about Miss Tims. When Lilian mentioned that she had been to see the old nurse Mrs Gladstone expressed no surprise but said, "It's a great mistake to go poking into others' business you've no call to."

"I thought it *was* my business," Lilian said by way of defence, but she got no answer.

The next day a picture postcard arrived from Roy. It showed the large oil refinery at Fawley on Southampton Water. He had added wisps of vapour to the pictured machinery, streaming out over the water and marked 'smell.' All he wrote was 'The prevailing wind takes it away from us, thanks be. Love Roy.'

Lilian immediately wrote a long letter in answer to this. She had no news except her failed researches and their consequent uneasiness. She was so little satisfied with this letter that she hid it away in her bedroom, uncertain whether to send it or not. As she did so, she felt another wave of depression pass over her. Though she had written her letter in her small office on paper headed with the practice address and the names of the partners, she had not dared to leave it in her office table drawer. She knew she was watched. She knew too much altogether. Only the dregs of her former affection for her uncle and a certain obstinate refusal to be cowed, kept her at her post.

97

This attitude was reinforced at the end of the week, during the drug addicts' clinic. Dr William kept the cards for these patients himself, but he expected Lilian, as well as Mrs Gladstone, to keep the waiting room under control. No queue jumping, no murderous quarrels, no disgusting collapses, no gate-crashing. It was astonishing what a calming effect a white overall had on these drop-outs, even if it was worn by a solitary girl of slim build and gentle appearance. Not to mention Mrs Gladstone's robust presence and sharp tongue.

Lilian did not spend much of the time in the waiting room, but she opened the inner door to look in from time to time, encourage those who were obviously sick, restrain the noisy or the weeping, dismiss the would-be belligerent with a warning that if they continued their shouting and abuse outside the house she would ring for the police. This warning always brought the rest of the patients to her side with various offers of ways to "take the sod apart". Nothing more was ever needed.

On this particular occasion, at one of her entrances, a tall lad got up quietly and approached her.

"Will it be Dr Cartwright in there?" he asked in a low voice.

"I'm afraid not," Lilian answered. "Dr Cartwright was only doing locum. He's gone away now to another practice. He won't be here again."

"He was very good to me," the boy said. "He started getting me unhooked. There was a bit of a row over it, I understand."

"Yes," Lilian remembered. "You were found . . ." Mustn't mention the police, you dim wit, she told herself, hurrying on, ". . . and went into hospital, didn't you?"

"I went home and into a place near there. I can't see Dr Cartwright, then?"

She remembered forwarding his letter to Roy. The latter could not have answered it.

"Look," she said. "You wrote to him, didn't you?" She drew him outside the waiting room door, to the accompaniment of uninhibited whistles and words of obscene encouragement. "I forwarded that letter to his new address. I'll do that again, if you like."

"Your name is . . .?" The young man looked pleased and satisfied. "I'll need your name to write to you."

"Lilian Bartlett. And yours is Giles Long. I remember. Come to my office and I'll give you an envelope with my name on."

That evening when Dr Williams had finished his late supper and gone to bed she got out her unfinished letter to Roy and added an account of the drug patient's arrival and what followed.

"You may have started a real cure," she wrote. "Though I know it's pretty rare. I hope he does write to you. He doesn't know your address, but you may want to see him."

She finished the letter with suitable, cool formalities and posted it the next morning herself when she went out shopping.

Roy's answer to this came by return of post. He wrote that he would come to London at his next week-end off duty and would arrange to see the dope case again then at his uncle's home. One of the more hopeful signs, he added, was that the lad had gone back to his parents when his intensive treatment was finished, though he did not want to stay there permanently. He must be given every possible encouragement. He, Roy, wanted above anything else to see her again. Would she have lunch with him? He had a great deal to tell her.

They met at a small restaurant in Bloomsbury. To Lilian's surprise and immediate mortification she found a third person already established at the table. This was a middle-aged man with greying hair and a pleasant smile. A friendly soul, but superfluous, she told herself, angrily. But her feeling changed at once when the stranger was introduced to her as Mr Markson.

"You must be Tom's father," she said, not knowing quite how to go on. But the expression of concern on her face quite sufficiently conveyed her compassion to Mr Markson, who said quietly, "I am, and I thank you for your sympathy. I did not find anything of the sort in Dr Phillips's attitude."

"They met at the inquest," Roy explained. "Mr Markson will tell us about it later." He signed to the waiter and went on, "I've ordered, Lil. I hope you don't mind, but I made an appointment with young—you know who—for this afternoon. I must be back in Southampton before eight. My bosses think I'm on the water. I'd like it to stay that way, so they'll expect me to be back at the Mellishes before dark."

"It's dark by six now, with this idiotic summer time going all through the winter," Lilian reminded him.

"You're right, but I shouldn't think they'd fuss till after eight."

The trivial conversation went on, with Mr Markson silent, eating slowly, waiting for Roy to give him an opening to begin questioning Lilian about his son's work in the practice at Azalea Road.

She could not tell him very much. Tom had been with them for a little over two years, as a trainee assistant.

"But that is the position he had in Overton," Mr Markson exclaimed. "Which is the truth? That he worked for Dr Armitage for a year and then transferred to London, then back to Armitage for only one week before he disappeared..."

"While I was engaged as his locum for a month," Roy put in. "As I told you," he added, turning to Markson.

"I just don't understand," Lilian insisted. "Please tell me exactly what came out at the inquest."

She looked from one to the other of the two men. It was Mr Markson who explained. There had been another adjournment, he told her. The cause of death was drowning, but certain marks at the wrists and ankles, though not conclusive, owing to the length of time the body had been in the water, did suggest ligatures.

"You mean he may have tied his own ankles and wrists before...before..."

100

"Going into the water. Yes, suicides did that, the coroner explained."

"On the other hand, so do murderers," said Roy.

"Which is the explanation I prefer," Mr Markson agreed. "But I can see there is no proof without much more evidence."

He turned to Lilian.

"Tell me about my son as you knew him, Miss Bartlett. Dr Armitage was kind, very polite, but told me nothing. Dr Phillips I do not trust at all."

"Who does?" said Roy, but Lilian frowned at him and he did not try to elaborate his beginning.

She gave Mr Markson as full an account as she could of Tom's two years work in the Azalea Road practice. He was very clever, very conscientious, she said. Most of the patients liked him very much. Only a few of the older private patients, accustomed to Dr Williams, refused to see him or be visited by him.

"They did that to me," Roy went on, trying to avoid the inevitable conclusion.

"They did it because he was half Indian and looked it," Mr Markson said quietly. "He'd be taken as wholly Indian in this country, I expect. At home he had trouble too sometimes because they said he was an Englishman. His mother is Indian, or rather I should say now, Pakistani. When I married her in the late thirties she was Indian and became British by marrying me. All my children are British. There was no trouble over Tom studying medicine in this country."

Lilian went on with her account. She spoke carefully, to soften or suppress the fairly constant snags that arose for Tom in some cases from prejudice, in others from the opposite, an eager wish to enlist him in various groups and societies for the improvement of immigrant conditions and housing in those parts of London where Pakistanis and other groups had settled or wished to settle.

"He wanted to learn his job," Mr Markson said, as she paused, wondering what else she could tell him. "He was interested in the immigrant social position in regard to

101

health, but he had no real sympathy with their aims. He wanted to come back to Bombay to practice in his own country."

"You think of Pakistan as your own country?" Roy asked.

"I've worked there in my present business for forty years," answered Mr Markson. "When I went out there were two partners, one English the other native. That had been so since it began, after the Mutiny. The English one died and I was promoted. I married the boss's daughter. A standard move, isn't it? Anyway, one I've never regretted."

"I suppose you are head of the firm now?" Roy said, hoping to get away from the story of Tom in England, for he did not want Lilian to give away too many of Azalea Road's dubious activities.

Mr Markson nodded.

"My eldest son came into the business with me when the old man died," he said. "He's six years older than Tom—was."

They all sat silent at this, until Mr Markson, turning again to Lilian asked, "Did you know Tom at all well, Miss Bartlett? I mean, personally? Did he ever take you out . . . Or anything?"

Tom, poor lad, Mr Markson explained, had often written high praise of Lilian, seldom a letter that did not describe her goodness, her beauty, his anxiety for her in the unhealthy atmosphere of the house with the ridiculous name. Azalea Road. But it had been Mafeking Terrace. Before the Council Estate wiped out those houses and the surgery annexe had been built.

"Yes, that's right. Tom used to come in to dinner with Uncle James and me about once a week," Lilian answered, dodging the question. "He was very interested in the history of the practice. Our house and the others of that group were built just after the Boer War. That's why the older ones have funny names like Spion Cop and Ladysmith."

"And Mafeking Terrace," Mr Markson said, smiling.

102

"He told me in his letters. He often mentioned you in his letters, Miss Bartlett, as I said just now."

She lowered her eyes to avoid showing him her mild embarrassment. Tom had never made any advances whatever, mild or otherwise. But then she had given him no opportunity.

"He always went out when he was off duty," she said. "I don't know where to exactly. I always thought it must be to friends from —from India."

"Tell me quite openly, Miss Bartlett. Did you think of him as wholly alien, wholly Indian?"

She was distressed now, not knowing how to answer him.

"I don't think I thought about him like that—I mean *racially*. There are always people from abroad around London, especially in medicine, I mean. In hospitals and practices, lots of them. Doctors or students, visiting here or there to learn. It never seems strange, I mean. One doesn't . . ."

"Don't worry," Mr Markson said. "Cartwright here says just the same. I understand. I must go further. I see Tom did not confide in you, Miss Bartlett. But he had friends. That I do know. Friends, if you can call them that. I think some of them were enemies. I must look for them among the people who tried to make him join their crazy societies. Their anti-British, trouble-making groups. You cannot then tell me of any enemies Tom may have had, Miss Bartlett?"

"Only one. Dr Bernard Phillips."

She had said it without realising where it would lead. She heard Roy exclaim *"No!"* and Mr Markson at once urge her to explain. She knew she ought not to have spoken, but it was too late to withold a reasonable explanation. And she had one, the same story, the same attempt that Phillips had made on Roy.

Having protested at once but without success, the latter heard her out in silence and when she had finished, remained silent until Mr Markson turned to him and said, "You did not tell me this."

103

"I wasn't in it. I only had it from Lil."

"Didn't you believe her?"

"Of course I believed her. That doesn't alter the fact it was hearsay, does it? Even if it seemed to link my experience with his."

Mr Markson began to say, "Do the police . . ." but a look from Roy checked him and he altered what he was about to say into "Don't you think you should tell the police . . . ?"

Lilian was not deceived.

"I think Roy may have done so already. He—at any rate his uncle, who is a barrister, knows a very high-up character at Scotland Yard. Hull—Commander Hull—isn't that it, Roy?"

"You would not object to repeating what you have told me to this Mr Hull or anyone else?" Mr Markson asked.

"I should certainly object to my uncle being brought into any sort of publicity," she said stoutly, but quaking inside when she thought of Dr Phillips's likely reaction.

"It is more important than that," Mr Markson said. "But I think I agree with you that Dr Phillips cannot be the chief enemy my poor son discovered. All the same I shall not leave England until I have found him, until I have proved that he killed Tom, who would never, I am convinced, never have committed suicide. You may tell Miss Bartlett, Cartwright. I am going now. I have a long list of names to visit."

He shook hands with Lilian, thanking her warmly for her sympathy and her substantial help. He shook hands with Roy, thanking him for an excellent lunch. He went away with rapid strides, without looking back, leaving the young people together.

"More coffee?" Roy said, feeling the pot to see if it was still warm.

"Yes, please. I certainly need it."

"Me too."

"What did he mean, all that about enemies?" she asked presently.

"You put your clumping great foot into it there, didn't you? Ouch!"

Lilian, who had planted her heel on his instep under the table, smiled and repeated her question.

"About enemies? Well, it looks as if your Tom Markson had got himself mixed up in shady happenings in the immigration racket. No, I don't know anything definite and I wouldn't be able to tell you if I did."

"Because you got this from your Uncle Killick?"

"Clever girl. Now can we leave the subject of suicide or mayhem and talk about ourselves?"

"Are you being callous or just showing off?"

"Purely selfish. Look, I want you to see my new practice. I shall have another free Saturday in a fortnight's time. Can you get off for the weekend? The Pratts—you remember Clare Pratt put me on to my landlords, the Mellishes—well, Clare could give you a bed and breakfast over Saturday night. You must come, Lil."

It was very tempting. Roy was looking at her with an expression of tender eagerness that melted her always lonely heart. It was sweet of him to have made lodging arrangements already and put them to her to explain that he wasn't just making a very cagey pass.

"I'd love to," she said slowly. "But I wouldn't be able to have the car."

"The train's all right. Cheap weekend ticket probably. I can meet you at the station. If it's a fine day we can go sailing from Hamble."

More and more tempting. But she thought of Uncle James, all alone on Saturday night after the drug clinic. No one to give him his supper, no one to help him to bed. He always drank himself silly after the Saturday drug clinic.

"It would have to be just for the day," she said, regretfully. "I daren't leave Uncle James all on his own with no one to get his supper or his breakfast on Sunday. I'd have to get back by ten at the latest."

Roy did not argue. He understood her burden, her

responsibility, her unbreakable loyalty to the old man who had let her down over and over again.

"Right," he said cheerfully. "Saturday only this time. After all it *is* October. About the end of the season really. We may not sail at all if it's wet or blowing, but we'll have a bash if we can."

"What in?" Lilian asked nervously. "I haven't done much ever."

"Not to worry. At the moment I share a friend's dinghy."

So the visit was fixed and they left the restaurant together. Lilian was so happy she characteristically remembered Mr Markson's set face as he left them.

"Poor Mr Markson," she murmured.

"Who? Oh, Markson? Yes. I could have wished him miles away when he asked me to let him meet you."

"When was that?"

"Before the inquest. Armitage introduced us outside the court."

Lilian went back to Azalea Road in high spiritis which were not damped by her uncle's querulous complaints that night at having to answer the telephone in her absence.

"You must get another locum," she told him."You know you and Dr Phillips can't possibly manage by yourselves."

"You don't know what you're talking about," he answered, peevishly.

"I think I do," she told him, too happy, too hopeful for her future to notice the strange look he gave her then and the long silences between them for the rest of the evening.

Chapter 11

The dinghy at Hamble was not at all intimidating, Lilian found. Not one of the fast racing kinds where the crew lay on a board outside the boat with his head practically in the water. She had foreseen something of the kind for herself, unless she was to be merely a passenger crouched in the middle of the boat, very uncomfortable and feeling in the way.

Roy's dinghy or rather his half-share dinghy, was a solid little craft, the sort of thing to take children in for short trips, reasonably stable, not listing far, not sailing very fast, either.

"I wouldn't have time for the class stuff," Roy explained. "I just like being on the water, always have. And under sail, not power," he added, as he pushed the dinghy into the water and held it while Lilian embarked carefully. As she did so the wash from a speed boat driving much too fast up the river rocked the boat so that she staggered but managed to sit down inside the hull instead of in the water. Roy, splashed up to the waist, said fiercely, "See what I mean? They ought to give the bloody things a marina of their own. They've no business to come among civilised craft."

Lilian laughed. Roy pushed away from the hard, stepping quickly on board as he did so, dropped the centreboard, gathered in the sheets and they were away, slipping quickly down the river helped by the falling tide and a very gentle breeze from the north. He kept the dinghy on the shoreward side of the line of moored yachts. They were mostly deserted. A few had owners on board, sorting out and piling on deck all the blankets, sleeping bags and other movable fittings that they would take home to store in a dry place for the winter.

The sun shone low in the sky, a glittering orange-gold

track on the water as they moved gently out into the winding open mouth of the river to join Southampton Water. A mild swell began to swing the little boat up and down, slapping her bows and running with a faint hiss to her stern.

"Like to take her?" Roy asked, offering the tiller.

"Not yet," Lilian told him." I wouldn't know how with all this traffic. Do we have to keep strictly inside the posts?"

"Not in this. If we pull up the centreboard we don't draw more than an inch or so. But it does dry out both sides, as you can see."

On their left going down Lilian did see there was hardly any water on the mud, with gulls and cormorants wading about. To the right a bank of mud showed clear of the little waves.

"It'll turn in a few minutes now," Roy said. "When we come back we can cut the corners."

"Where are we going?"

He said carefully, not looking at her, watching his sail and the shipping, "If you really have to get that six-thirty train we'd better not go too far. This wind might pick up a bit but it'll probably drop altogether by mid-afternoon. I don't fancy rowing all the way. I mean, the Island is out for this time."

"I've never actually been to it," Lilian said wistfully, looking across to the misty shores of the Isle of Wight.

"Next time."

"I thought you said it was the end of the season?"

"So it is. But a dinghy doesn't take much laying up. I expect we'll keep her going till the weather gets too foul."

This vague explanation did not encourage Lilian. 'Next time' had been a polite excuse for not taking her to Cowes, which did not look very far away across the Solent. They were just off Calshot by this time and had been sailing for a little less than an hour.

Roy looked at his watch and altered course so that they pointed towards the big refinery at Fawley.

"I'm going to make for Fawley," he said. "Wind and

108

tide against us at the moment. Watch how we go on that buoy. Black Jack, it's called."

"But it's red," Lilian objected.

"I know, but that's because it's a porthand mark," he answered. "Are you watching?"

She was not enlightened, but she was watching. They were still pointing at Fawley, they were sailing very nicely through the water, but Black Jack was going away from them in the direction of Southampton. In other words they were proceeding as fast as before in the direction of Cowes but at the same time moving into the track of a ferry crammed with passengers and cars.

Roy put the dinghy about again, pointing now back towards Warsash on the mainland opposite Hamble. As he had predicted the wind was freshening. Their adverse progress was held, but the waves grew and the spray with them.

Roy turned again when the ferry had passed.

"We'll have slack water in a few minutes now," he said. "I'll go up beyond Calshot and turn in towards the land there. It gets shallow but that doesn't matter. We'll sit on the mud and have lunch."

This manoeuvre was successful. In the wide shallow bay protected from the north by the refinery and from the south by the Calshot tongue of land, the dinghy with the centreboard pulled up sat square on the mud. Roy pulled out a haversack and took from it several plastic containers and a pair of binoculars.

"What are those for?" Lilian asked, setting out the lunch between them.

"Curiosity," Roy answered with a laugh. "All this shipping. Ah!"

He had the glasses trained on a fishing boat, black and old-fashioned, that had begun to move from its station near the opposite side of Southampton Water to one just outside the buoyed channel.

"Anything in particular?" Lilian asked, still occupied with the food.

"Not yet," Roy answered. He put the binoculars down beside him and turned to the sandwiches.

They ate in silence. There was no need for words, Lilian felt. She was happier than she had been since the day Roy had first taken her out. The visit to his uncle and aunt had been interesting, but a bit nerve-racking to some-one who went out as little as herself and only to see friends of her own age. All or nearly all the Williams' friends had dropped them after Aunt Emily's death. Certainly all the women friends and most of their husbands. Only a few old medical buddies of poor Uncle James still came to see him sometimes and spent an hour or two with him in the study. She herself took no part in such visits. Her last outing with Roy in London had been marred by the presence of Mr Markson. It had been too painful on account of poor Tom, the mysery of his sad death, the lurking terror that lay behind it. So this was only the second time she had been really alone with Roy, in glorious late sunshine, a gentle cool breeze, the trees be-hind them beginning to glow with their autumn red and gold, the sky a cloudless blue, the water reflecting the reeds further back towards the shore. Alone with Roy, invited to be alone with him, eating the gorgeous sand-wiches his new landlady presumably had made for them both.

Alone indeed, for as the minutes passed it became clear, very clear, that his attention was not for her at all, but solely on the movements, very pleasant to watch, but wholly unimportant, of the shipping in the deeper waters between the two shores.

"Here she comes!" Roy said excitedly.

The tall bows of an ocean liner moved into view from behind the buildings on Calshot Point. She was travelling at a very reduced speed, but still much faster than any of the sailing craft and most of the motor boats, except those that were suddenly aware of her presence and her inexor-able approach across their path.

They all took evading action; some neatly because they knew what they were doing, some clumsily, even danger-ously, because they lacked any kind of seamanship. Among the latter would appear to be the old fishing boat. When the liner passed there she was, plunging up and down in the big ship's wake, some of the men who had been holding rods and lines over the side winding in the latter, others reaching overboard to disentangle their tackle that had been swept together by the violent movement.

Roy handed the glasses to Lilian.

"Have a look," he said. He turned from her to sweep the remains of their meal into the containers and back into the haversack.

"What at?" she asked.

"The fishing boat. Recognise anyone on board?"

"I can't get it focussed. Oh, now it's better. Why did they get so close to the liner?"

"Why indeed? No one you know?"

"Why should there be? You did mean the fishing boat? Not the big ship?"

"I did. It doesn't matter. I just wondered."

"Why? Did you?"

"No. At least . . . No."

"Roy! What *is* all this?"

He snatched back the glasses. A smart motor cabin cruiser was roaring out of the Hamble churning up a big bow wave and leaving a foam-flecked wake and a wash that bounced every small craft round it and rocked several larger yachts that were making the best of the very light airs.

"Now," Roy said, giving Lilian back the binoculars. "One quick look at that fantastic outfit. The white horror charging out of the Hamble. I thought so. Give!" He snatched at the glasses again. *"I thought so!"*

Lilian was affronted.

"What is all this?" she cried again angrily. "What's going on? Quiet lunch my foot! Whatever you're doing you had it all worked out before hand. Only I don't see why . . ."

She broke off because she had been staring about her while Roy kept his gaze fixed on the white cabin cruiser that had just spun about to float quietly past the fishing boat, almost touching it but not quite. Near enough for an exchange of words, angry perhaps, perhaps merely hearty. Too far away to see the real expressions on their faces.

"Roy!" Lilian was on her knees at his side, jerked there by the dinghy's movement as she leaned across to speak to him. "Roy, we're . . ."

"Afloat? Fine. Lil, my darling, snatch up that oar and stick it overboard upright—to find how deep it is. I must just . . ."

She did as she was told. At least it was a combined action at last, even if she had no idea what it was all about.

"It's half way up," she reported.

"Once more."

"Ow! I nearly dropped it. No bottom here."

He slipped the strap of the binoculars round his neck, dropped the centreboard, pulled up the sails and in a very few seconds the little boat was moving again, away from the shore, out into the channel and this time with the wind behind them, defeating the inflowing tide as they made their way back to the mouth of the Hamble.

When they appeared to be settled on a course Roy, after entrusting her with the tiller, put away the binoculars in their case. He stuffed this into the haversack and the whole into the small locker in the bows. As he sat back she asked, in a deliberately long-suffering voice, "*Now* will you tell me what all this has been in aid of?"

He laughed.

"All what?"

"Oh Roy, don't be *maddening*! All this—coming out here, parking where we did, watching the boats, that black one in particular and the white speedboat . . ."

"The liner, Lil, you've forgotten the liner. Did you notice any of the people lined up on the decks?"

She frowned, trying to remember, but she had been concerned with their lunch, she had only glanced up now and then.

"No," she answered. "Not really. Where had it come from?"

"Cherbourg, today. Before that the Atlantic, the Cape of Good Hope, the Indian Ocean, Bombay."

The penny droped.

"India!"

"Pakistan. And don't say it's the same thing. You met Markson didn't you?"

"Roy, is all this something to do with Tom?"

"Wait and see. I'll tell you one thing, though. So that it won't be a surprise when we are back at Hamble. The two types on the white job. Did you get a good look at them?"

"Misty. I still can't focus it properly. Who were they?"

"My two bosses. Dr Armitage and Dr Thompson."

"No!"

"Sure thing. Look where you're going!"

He seized the tiller over her hand to bring the dinghy back on course and avoid a gybe.

"You take it," Lilian said, trying to free her hand.

"No. I like it like this."

He moved to sit beside her with his arm round her and his hand still over hers. But their combined weight on one side put them down too far and he scrambled back, but still imprisoned her hand.

"I didn't know all this would blow up when I asked you down," he explained.

"Didn't you?" She tried to add a note of indifference but failed. The result was a shaky sound, not at all what she wanted.

"Honestly no. Only this morning, when I reminded Armitage I was off for the day and he said he thought of going with Thompson for a short spin in his new cabin cruiser."

"So what?"

"So I remembered Markson had given me a list of dates of arrivals here of ships from Bombay and Calcutta. I looked it up and this was one of them."

"How convenient. But what has it to do with you taking me for a sail?"

"Lil *please!* I told you we might not sail at all if the

113

weather was lousy. I meant it and I wouldn't have taken you. But it's been perfect, hasn't it?"

"Have you really had time to notice that?"

His face darkened. He took his hand away at which she repeated, "You take it." They had nearly reached the buoy at the entrance to the river. She dared not try to sail up it by herself.

After a few minutes Roy said, "You know I'd tell you if I knew anything about this miserable business, don't you?"

She said coldly, "You'd far better not, hadn't you? I'm still one of the highly dubious lot at Azalea Road, aren't I? The people who tried to frame you and beat you up."

This was so exactly what Roy did think that he blushed violently and could find nothing convincing to refute it. But when Hamble came in sight again he muttered desperately, "You're very bitter, aren't you? Do you never trust anyone?"

That broke her. With tears running down her face she managed to say, "What do you expect? You've seen it all. Who could I trust? Who?"

He had put an arm out and pulled her close before she could go on, so she turned her face into his shoulder and cried there until she remembered where she was, sat back and began furiously to blow her nose and wipe her face.

Roy gave his full attention to conducting the dinghy up the river to the hard at Hamble. Before they reached it he said, without looking round at her, "My poor love, I'll make you trust me. You'll see. And to begin with the white devil has just wizzed past us back to her mooring. So we shall be walking up to the restaurant for tea when they reach the club house. Or just about."

"Have I got to meet them?"

"Better. Don't you think?"

She had left her handbag in Roy's car, but she had power and lipstick in her pocket and made an immediate rapid repair to her face. She had not attempted to make up her eyes that morning, suspecting rightly that blown spray would result in a hopeless mess. When she disem-

114

barked and had helped Roy to pull the dinghy up out of the water and stow the gear, he caught her close and inspected her face gravely before he kissed her.

"Full marks," he said. "I'm delighted to see your nose doesn't swell and go red when you cry."

"Ill-mannered oaf!"

"Bad-tempered bitch!"

They were both laughing too much to go on.

"This is where the four-letter words start in the telly plays," Lilian began, but Roy stopped her.

"Straight ahead," he said. "With my new bosses. Do you see what I see?"

Dr Phillips, just stowing a parcel in the deep pocket of his light-coloured raincoat, was talking eagerly with Dr Armitage and Dr Thompson. It was the stout Thompson who noticed the young people approaching and hailed them jovially. Dr Phillips's face froze.

"Been out for a spin?" Thompson asked when the introductions were made.

"You too, I suppose?" Roy said calmly, taking Lilian's arm and squeezing it slightly to keep her silent. "I didn't see you."

"Where were you?" Dr Armitage asked coolly.

"Oh, we just wafted down towards Lee on the tide and tacked gently back when it turned. Suitable for beginners, eh, Lil?"

"Very," she said, smiling gently and added, "I think— tea—or I'll miss my train."

"Quite."

It all seemed to have gone off very well until they left the restaurant to find Dr Phillips waiting outside.

"I've got my car here, Lilian," he said. "Why not let me run you back? I'm going straight home."

She was horrified. Spoil this day which was already sinking into history as a golden event! Leave Roy with no opportunity to tell him . . .

"Thanks very much," she said as lightly as she could. "But I don't think . . ."

"Nonsense," Dr Phillips told her in the cold bossy

manner that always frightened her. "A straight drive for an hour and a half instead of traipsing round stations and trains and buses. Tell her, Cartwright. It's crazy to pass it up. Besides, I've one or two bits of practice business I want to talk over. Also your Uncle . . ."

"What about Uncle James?"

"He wasn't too good when I left. But I said I'd be back in good time. He told me you were spending the day in the country with friends."

"So I was," said Lilian. She turned to Roy, "Perhaps if Uncle James . . ."

He nodded. His face expressed indifference, complete lack of interest in her plans, her movements. They said goodbye with friendly thanks on both sides. Lilian walked to the car park with Dr Phillips, not looking back. Roy unlocked his own car, some distance away and took out Lilian's handbag. He had a brief look at the contents, then ran over to where Dr Phillips was adjusting the safety strap for Lilian.

"You nearly went off without this," Roy said.

Lilian, white-faced, thanked him. He waited until Dr Phillips drove away, then ran back to his own car and drove off in the opposite direction.

On the way back to Azalea Road Lilian said very little, which did not matter at all as Dr Phillips talked most of the time. The subject of his intermittent lecture was Roy. An irresponsible, unsatisfactory young man, deceptively modest and charming, which was only a cover for self-assurance and basic ignorance. Basically dishonest, too, as witness his behaviour that day.

"How?" Lilian managed to ask, cutting in out of sheer exasperation with this flow of lying nonsense.

"How? Surely that's obvious. He asked you down to go sailing with him when he knew perfectly well he would most likely be on duty today."

"He knew nothing of the sort. It was his weekend off duty. He only has one in three."

"Trainee assistants are supposed to be learning their job. They should be grateful for a whole weekend in four.

116

Take today. Armitage rang him up quite early to tell him he would be going out with Thompson. He found young Cartwright had already left. At nine-thirty in the morning."

"That's right. To meet my train from Waterloo at ten-five. But Dr Thompson knew he was going sailing."

"I suppose you told your uncle where you were going?"

She did not answer. She could not without being frankly rude and after all he was giving her a lift. She wished she had insisted upon going back by train. Roy had only to back her up, but he did exactly the opposite. Why?

Dr Phillips continued his lecture until they reached Azalea Road. The house seemed to be in darkness, but it was still only dusk outside, though the street lamps were on. Dr Phillips drew up in the road outside the front door. He frowned at the dark building.

"No light in the hall," he said.

Lilian did not hear him. She was already out of the car and running up the steps. She called out, "Thanks very much for the lift," as she turned the key in the lock and went in, shutting the door at once behind her. She too had noticed the darkness.

She found the hall switch, she went at once to the study. This room too was in darkness, no light, no fire. When she turned the switch she saw her uncle, lying back in his usual armchair. She spoke his name and went up to him to wake him.

But Uncle James was dead.

Chapter 12

Roy drove off in the direction of Southampton, avoiding any chance of overtaking his partners' car. He followed the sign posts on minor roads to Netley, where he had arranged to meet his uncle and Commander Hull outside the gates of Netley Abbey.

When he arrived he saw only one car in the appointed place and it was not Sir Henry's. Also it was empty. But he parked his own beside it, got out and looked about him. The Abbey was still open to the public until the end of October, he read on a board by the entrance, from two to five pm on Saturday and Sunday. He went up to the gates hoping to see the visitors, wondering if he ought to go in himself to avoid questions about his apparent loitering. But before he made up his mind the visitors walked out from behind the ruins and he saw that they were Uncle Harry and Commander Hull.

"You're early, Roy," the former said as they came through the official exit.

"Am I?" he answered. He had not bothered to look at his watch for a long time; too much was happening. So he said no more as they walked back to the parked cars.

"Get in with us," Commander Hull said, smiling. "Yes, it's mine. You wouldn't know it, of course."

So Roy told them exactly what he had done and how he had followed the motor cruiser back into the Hamble.

"I've got your camera binoculars, or long-distance camera or whatever you call it, in my car. Don't let me forget to give it to you."

"I won't forget," Hull assured him.

"I think I got a nice one of the chaps on the fishing boat handing something to Armitage. Thompson was driving the cruiser. At least one and I think both of the thugs

118

who went for me at Azalea Road were in the fishing boat."

"Were they indeed? Then I hope we'll be able to identify them."

"I asked Lil—Lilian Bartlett—if she recognised anyone, but she said no. I don't think she had focussed the glasses properly. I don't think she was pretending not to recognise."

Sir Henry was amused.

"That's not a very kind thing to say about Lilian. We thought she was far nicer than any of the last few young women you've brought along for meals."

Roy grew red. Though he shared his uncle's opinion and had begun to feel he might be falling for Lil in a really big way, he had been annoyed with her for expecting him to persuade her away from Dr Phillips. If she was really under that obvious rogue's influence, even in his power, he was not going to get any deeper in than he was already.

"You don't really think Lilian is working with this racket, do you?" Uncle Harry went on, more seriously. "Not knowingly or willingly?"

"I honestly don't know what to think," Roy answered.

Commander Hull said, "So what we've got is that something was passed, from a type you think you identify, to Dr Armitage. Did you see where it came from?"

"Unfortunately no. When the liner passed she was between us and the fishing boat. But they had moved conveniently out away from this side of Southampton Water. After she passed they were rocking up and down in her wake, making a great show of sorting out their lines, scooping about in the water, hanging overboard and so on. One of them could easily have picked up a small object dropped from the ship and floating."

"Quite."

"Then when you got back to Hamble you saw Dr Phillips talking to your two bosses," Sir Henry said, pushing on with the report. His nephew was making rather heavy weather of it, probably on account of the girl, he thought. That must account for his very early arrival at the rendez-

119

vous. He was supposed to have seen her on to her train first.

"Yes. There were some rather sour introductions all round. Phillips was tucking something into a coat pocket, or reaching for a handkerchief. I didn't see. Thompson asked us where we'd been and I said just floating down on the tide towards Lee and then floating back when it turned. I hope to God Lil remembers that."

"Hardly likely to," Hull said to Sir Henry, "if she hasn't been out here before. But probably Phillips wouldn't ask her where they went."

"He might ask her what they were doing."

"She might tell him at that," Roy suggested bitterly, but he did not really mean it.

The older men exchanged glances but said nothing.

"I'll get those binoculars," Roy said, "before I forget."

He was out of the car before Hull could stop him.

"There's no one about," Sir Henry said. "Not that it would matter if there were. He doesn't seem to have been followed."

"He wouldn't be—openly," Hull answered. "I'm not sure we ought to let him go any further with this thing, or not without warning him."

"Of what?"

The Commander sighed.

"The girl is a complication. She ought not to be left in that outfit with a totally unreliable alcoholic uncle and a crook medico. But she won't leave the uncle, that's for sure."

"I don't think Roy will leave *her,*" his uncle said. "He's never been like this before over a girl. Pleasant episodes— short and sweet—no regrets—no ill feelings. That's been the pattern so far as his father and I know."

"Which is only the tip of the iceberg, I don't mind betting. Here he is."

Roy handed the binoculars through the car window, but did not get in again.

"I think I'd better be getting along," he said. "My bosses know I had Lil with me. I think I told them I was seeing her on to a train after we'd had tea. There was only

Phillips outside when we left but he may have arranged with them already to take her up in his car. I want to get back at a reasonable time."

"You think things out clearly enough," Commander Hull said, smiling. "Perhaps you ought to come on the strength."

"Not on your nelly," Roy answered. "Medicine is my job, and I intend to do it when I have half a chance. That is when you two let me out of the situation you've put me in."

Sir Henry leaned forward.

"We *are* letting you out, Roy," he said. "Don't be annoyed because we encouraged you to take this job and the locum that *we* knew, but *you* didn't, went with it. The two practices have been under observation for some time. You wouldn't have been able to carry off all you've done to help if you'd known about it before hand."

"I wouldn't have gone within miles of them if I'd known the first thing."

"Exactly. But I think we can tell you it all had to do with Tom Markson's position and then his disappearance. He was a promising young doctor, determined to go back and serve his own country with the training he got here."

"So what?"

"So we are pretty sure he was murdered," Commander Hull intervened quietly. "We have evidence that points that way."

"From his father? He had lunch with me and Lil was there, too."

Roy remembered she had been less than enthusiastic over the way the conversation had clung to Tom Markson's fate. How deep was she in with the rogues or was she just an innocent stooge? It might be as well to cut loose now before . . .

"From Mr Markson," Commander Hull was saying. "But from fresh evidence you will know about quite soon."

"To hell with your evidence!" Roy said, furiously. "Cops and robbers, cloak and dagger! I'm through! Do your own dirty work from now on. I hope those photographs don't come out," he added, childishly.

The older men looked at him; quietly accepting these tantrums. In their several professions they were very well used to such outbursts.

Sir Henry said mildly, "I told you we did not want any more action from you, Roy. At the same time it might be as well to look out for another trainee job in say Devon or Cornwall."

"Thank you for nothing," Roy muttered angrily and stumped away to his car.

When he arrived at the Mellishes' house in Overton he found a pencil scrawl on the hall table which read 'Roy, we have gone up to the Pratts for the evening. Do come along if you have nothing better to do.'

It was friendly, it meant there would be no supper for him at home, but presumably that meal was included in the casual invitation. He decided to go. It would rub out the disappointments of the afternoon; also the unpleasantness of the interview at Netley Abbey with those two old cagey sleuth hounds. Also he could call in at the practice to ask Armitage if he was supposed to be on duty that evening as well as the following day.

So he had a bath to wash the salt off his skin and out of his hair, put on a suit to show willing in case Armitage or Thompson sprang a visit to a patient on him, and then drove along to the house where he parked in the doctors' lined parking space and rang the front door bell.

Mrs Hurst answered it. She stared at Roy for a few seconds before she said, "Well?" in her usual forbidding tone. She did not move aside to let him in, so he stayed where he was, staring back before he answered quietly, "I just called to let Dr Armitage know I was back in case there was anything he wanted me to do."

"Why should there be?"

This was doubly disconcerting. Roy explained that he was on his way to the Pratts and so called in on purpose instead of phoning.

"If Dr Armitage had phoned when I was on my way here, he would not have got an answer," he went on, patiently. "That's why I'm here."

He would have liked to add, "And I don't know why

I'm saying all this to you, you nosey old cow," but instead he repeated, "So if Dr Armitage is in, I'd like to have a word with him."

"He's not in," she answered grudgingly. "He was obliged to go out. Dr Thompson is taking the emergency calls until ten, when he will have them transferred to you."

"Thank you," Roy said in a cheerful voice as he turned away. "That's exactly what I wanted to know."

It was by no means all, but he knew he would get nothing more from Mrs Hurst. All the same it was most unlike Dr Armitage to go off again after he'd taken a rather unusual spin in the cruiser with Dr Thompson. It meant that the practice was unattended for several hours. Or was it? Probably some other local doctor had agreed to take any calls. It was easier, friendlier, over that sort of thing in the country practices. Or so he had been told by friends who had settled, by preference, as far from London as they could get, without being bogged down in an industrial slum.

A cheerful noise greeted him as he rang the bell at the Pratts' door; young voices, children's happy yells, the Pratt dog barking its head off.

"Excuse the shindy," Joe Pratt shouted above the noise. "Come in, come in!"

The din quietened as Roy went into the sitting room. The source of the noise was obvious. The two men had been competing in building towers of bricks, brought along by the Mellish boy, who was three. They were building against time with a limit of five minutes. Naturally their towers fell frequently. The object was to have the tallest standing at the end of the time allowed. Roy had arrived when George Mellish's tower had survived Joe's by one second with a half-brick taller in height.

"He practices at home," Joe complained.

"Time to put the kids down," Clare said. "They've had extra already."

Their mothers took them away to bed, the visitors in sleeping bags until their parents took them home in the back of their estate car.

Roy's tension left him in this most relaxed, normal and

cheerful atmosphere. He was put in an armchair with a drink. The three men chatted about things in general while the women settled their children and then began to get the supper on the table from the oven where it had been cooking quietly on its own. The whole evening was a demonstration of easy domestic happiness, Roy decided, quite charmed by the experience. The bright side, he told himself, later cynically wondering how many rows they had per week, how many heart searchings, how much mental and physical exhaustion. Don't be a pompous idiot, he told himself, putting away his car at the side of the Mellishes' house.

He had left the party early so as to be ready by ten o'clock for any emergency calls that might come in. So the house was still in darkness, but his mood was very different from when he came back from seeing Uncle Harry and the Commander. He was singing cheerfully as he went in. He switched on the hall and staircase lights, leaving them burning because Nancy Mellish had asked him to do so. He looked at his watch, saw the time was two minutes to ten. So he ran upstairs to his own room to put on his portable radio to hear the weather forecast.

Much the same as today, he heard. He flung himself into the small armchair George had lent him the day he arrived. When the news began he could not be bothered to get up and stop it. Almost at once he was sitting forward, gripping the arms of the chair.

'In the course of the last twenty-four hours two more bodies have been washed ashore between Bridport and Lyme Regis,' the quiet voice said. 'Taken together with the three found in the same area over the last two weeks and like them apparently of Indian or Pakistani nationality, this may be a clue to the mystery of the five crew members of the *Antigone* who apparently deserted their ship three weeks ago after she docked at Southampton. Police inquiries continue. Soccer results...'

Roy switched off and sat back, thinking. Three weeks ago, no, four weeks ago now, Tom Markson disappeared, deserting both the practices he had worked in. His body, too, turned up drowned. But in Southampton Water, not

124

Lyme Bay. He too came to England from Pakistan, though his father was English, London born. Was there any connection? There had to be. Why had he himself given up reading newspapers since he started real practice? No time, chiefly. Easier to use radio. When had the first three bodies turned up? Why had his bosses never said anything about them or about the inquiry for the deserters?

Why should they? It was not a bad way of getting into England. As ship's crew on shore leave, all quite legal and in order. Then just travel to the Midlands or further north and disappear. In that case why turn up drowned between Bridport and Lyme Regis? If they got ashore with no fuss why appear now as wrecked flotsam from the sea?

Wrecked! That must supply some answers. From what broken sinking vessels had they been thrown? And why, again why, were they at sea?

Roy managed to listen to the news at one o'clock the next day but there was no mention of the Lyme Bay bodies. At six he was working in the surgery which lasted that evening until after eight, with one new case for him of considerable interest that put the other mystery totally out of his mind. A medical mystery this one. How was it that an intelligent, skilled man, accustomed to using his brain in a clear, logical fashion, could fail to notice and question certain symptoms and signs of trouble in his own body? The answer, of course, was fear. He had refused to notice because he feared the answer.

Was fear also the answer to that other problem? The ten o'clock news merely aggravated the question. The drowned bodies had not been identified, but evidence had come to hand of certain wreckage thrown up a few weeks ago on Chesil Beach at Portland, perhaps of a raft or a dinghy, just planks, broken and torn by the recent gales, it was thought. The conclusion drawn from this was that the deserting Pakistani crew members were not involved, but there had been a failed attempt at an illegal immigrant landing.

Very likely, Roy thought. Which clears up nothing whatever. And leaves the question of Tom Markson's death precisely where it was.

Chapter 13

When Lilian had recovered a little from the first shock of finding her uncle dead in his chair, she looked at the table beside him and saw near the usual bottle and glass an envelope addressed to 'dear Lilian with love and apology'.

A suicide letter if ever there was one, she decided, putting it at once into the pocket of her slacks. Poor Uncle James. She had loved him very much as a child and though she had been disgusted and often furious over his uncontrolled drinking she had still loved him, or at least had determined to look after him.

Had she neglected this self-imposed duty, the promise she had made to her wholly admirable Aunt Emily? Ought she to have stayed at home today and perhaps saved Uncle James this time? She had no illusions about the probable future had she been successful. He never accepted outside help or attempted a cure of his vice. Once an alcoholic reached the stage of despair, when he believed his only escape was through death, he usually managed to bring it off, unless he was already so ill that his body gave up before he could achieve his desire by deliberate means. There had been patients she had known who had met their end in one or other of these ways.

Looking sadly again at her uncle's livid face her tears began to fall. She touched his hand, but drew back again instantly, shaking, revolted by the icy-cold, wooden state of the fingers that had always been warm soft and gentle when they touched her.

But this renewed shock brought her back to reality, back from her self-accusation and her self-consoling memories. Uncle James was dead: he had died alone and unexpectedly. What was the first thing she must do? Get help, of course.

With her acquired knowledge that such crises demanded official aid and meant an inquest, she thought of the coroner and someone her uncle always spoke of as the 'coroner's officer'. Well, that was a policeman, wasn't it? Then ring up the police, ring up 999.

There was a telephone on the desk at the other side of the room. She walked across to it and had picked up the receiver and begun to dial when the door of the study opened and Dr Phillips walked in. With a sharp exclamation of anger he strode across to her, snatched the receiver from her hand and slammed it back on the cradle.

Lilian shrank away, appalled. Not so much at his violence, which was sufficiently frightening, as at his total disregard of the dead man in the chair. Did he know already that Uncle James was dead? If so, why had he not told her? If not, why was it important to stop her telephoning? Did he guess that she wanted to call the police? Or at any rate someone other than himself?

This gave her the clue to what her immediate behaviour must be.

"Why?—Why?..." she stammered, finding it easy enough to pretend astonishment. "I thought you'd gone home! I was trying to call you! Uncle..."

Taking no further notice of her Dr Phillips had moved to the chair and bent over his dead colleague. When she spoke he looked round, his face quite expressionless.

"You found him like this—dead?" he asked.

"Of course. But he was alive this morning when I left. He seemed better than usual, then."

"He must have had a sudden heart attack," Dr Phillips said, calmly.

"All alone...and..." She began to move towards the door.

"Stay where you are."

The voice was so menacing and he had moved so suddenly across her path that she stood still, fighting down a sudden panic. But she knew now what she had to do. Wait obediently until this man was out of the house, then collect Uncle James's papers and records and her own possessions and leave Azalea Road herself for ever.

So she stayed. She crept to a chair and sat down with her head between her knees, fighting off the faintness that had come over her suddenly. She heard Dr Phillips speaking on the phone, evidently to Dr Waters. That must be the anaesthetist who was sometimes called in to assist at St Helen's. He was to come round at once, Dr Williams was ill.

When Dr Phillips had finished the call Lilian sat up again. Dr Waters was not a particularly nice little man, but he was harmless or had always seemed so. At any rate he would stand between her and Dr Phillips. She would not be alone in the house with an enemy.

"Waters is coming round," Dr Phillips said. "He will do what is necessary. And now will you tell me what you were doing when I very fortunately stopped you. Very fortunately for you and for all of us."

"I don't know what you mean," she said.

"You were dialling 999. That is not my number. You were not calling me."

"An ambulance," she said, desperately. "Hospital."

"But he was dead. You thought your uncle had committed suicide, didn't you?"

"I thought it might be that."

"Why? I don't see any proof of it? No letter, or anything of that sort?"

Lilian thought quickly. She felt sure Dr Phillips had discovered the death before he left for Southampton. So he must have seen the letter then. So why leave it there, if he was going to suggest a heart attack?

"There *was* a letter," she said. "That is why I decided it was suicide."

He stared at her.

"I will read it now," she said, taking it from her pocket. "I will give it to Dr Waters when he comes."

She opened it slowly and read. It was short, trite, a brief statement of his intention to end his useless life. He repeated the apology on the envelope. He repeated his love and signed it your affectionate Uncle Jim.

She had never in her life called him Uncle Jim.

"That will be Waters," Dr Phillips said as the house bell rang. "I'll bring him in."

The letter was not from Uncle James, then, though the writing was an excellent forgery. Perhaps Uncle James had written it some time ago and left it waiting for the moment when his courage grew large enough to get him started on that final act. But at no time would he sign himself Jim. Looking closely again at the letter Lilian thought she could detect a difference in the writing. But as she had never seen him write Jim but always James it was not possible to swear to it.

Very slowly she put the letter back into the envelope. She got to her feet, holding it out to Dr Waters as he came into the room, followed by Dr Phillips.

"You must take this, Dr Waters," she said. "The coroner will want it, won't he?"

Dr Waters took the envelope reluctantly. He was puzzled.

"I thought you said—heart," he began, but Dr Phillips stopped him.

"I didn't offer a diagnosis at all," he said. "I said—ill."

"Yes," Lilian agreed. "But Dr Phillips suggested heart to me—earlier. Before—well, before I read the letter."

She saw them exchange glances and again a sick feeling of helplessness flooded her and left her trembling.

"What will you do now?" she asked Dr Waters, knowing that tears were again running down her face but quite unable to stop crying.

"I shall call an ambulance," the little man said, "to have him transferred to the mortuary. I shall then get in touch with the coroner personally. That is required legally, I'm afraid."

"I thought so," Lilian said, shakily. "There will have to be an inquest, won't there?" she added, looking at Dr Phillips who was frowning at the unscreened window.

Lilian went over to pull the curtains. She then moved to the desk, opened it, took the key from a small drawer at the back, closed and locked the desk and turning said to Dr Waters, "Will you be staying till the ambulance comes, because I would like to go to my room and change. I don't want to be seen like this—casual—enjoying . . ." She could not go on, but Dr Waters understood.

"Of course I'll stay," he said. He looked at his watch. "They won't be long. I'll let you know."

She thanked him. Dr Phillips did not hold the door open for her, though he was near it, but she did not expect good manners from him. He usually treated her as an inferior, an amateur secretary, a hanger-on in the household, useful because they did not pay her a salary, though she appeared in the expenses of the practice for income tax purposes. Uncle James gave her a small allowance which he called pin money. Now . . .

She did not allow herself to wonder what would happen now, except that her resolve held more firmly than ever. Which was to leave Azalea Road as soon as, in decency, she could.

She locked the door of her room and went to her own desk which she had kept locked since she discovered the partners had read her letter from Roy. From a drawer in the desk she took out a letter Uncle James had given her at about the time Roy joined the practice. He had told her not to open it until his death. When she had protested that this would not be for years ahead he had smiled at her and said, "Do you really think so?" At which she had kissed him with tears in her eyes and begged him not to leave her alone in the world. "Not willingly," he had answered, still smiling.

Remembering this as she took out the envelope she grew more sure than ever that suicide was not the answer to his death. At present she could do nothing. But Dr Waters would not dare now to hush up the death. Besides 'they', having forged a suicide note, wanted an inquest, perhaps wanted to foist on to a dead man crimes for which 'they' were really responsible.

She opened the envelope. It did not seem to have been tampered with. It held a key wrapped in a sheet of writing paper on which Uncle James had written, 'Open the bottom drawer of the chest of drawers in my bedroom. You will find diaries and papers that relate to the whole of my career and account for my failure. I wish I had never been born. Forgive me for all the trouble I have given you and believe that I sincerely love you as the daughter I never had. My will is with my solicitors, Grant and Simmonds, Holborn. Your worthless but loving Uncle James.'

Proof and double proof of the forgery, Lilian thought, in the full rush of grief that burst upon her at these bitter words from a broken man.

She changed her slacks for a dark grey skirt and a black polo-necked sweater. She threaded the key and also her bedroom key on to a piece of ribbon and having locked her room from the outside hung the ribbon about her neck inside her sweater and went downstairs again.

There was no one in the hall. She tried the door of the study, not altogether surprised to find it locked. She went into the drawing room, this time surprised to find the air quite warm as she pushed open the door. Dr Phillips was there, sitting forward on a chair he had drawn up close to the electric fire, all its three bars glowing.

He looked up at her, but without speaking.

"Has Dr Waters . . . ? Have they . . . ?"

"The ambulance has taken your uncle to the mortuary. Waters has spoken to the constable who is on duty for the coroner. He has explained to him that you are too shocked to answer questions at once. Being a reasonably sentimental copper, he agreed to that. Especially as you have been away all day and could only tell him of your discovery made at the same time as me."

"A little before!" Lilian exclaimed indignantly.

"At the same time," he insisted. "There was a letter addressed to you, which you opened and passed to Waters, who has now given it to the officers of the law."

He spoke, as he so often did, in heavy sneering tones, in pompous, self-conceited words. Lilian was sickened, but she said nothing. An idea, prompted by a certain amount

131

of noise outside the house, had come to her. She ignored Dr Phillips's speech and went to the window, noticing that he had drawn these curtains also.

"I've just remembered," she said. "The drug clinic! They must be waiting! You'll have to take it, won't you?"

He sprang to his feet.

"What are you saying?"

"The junkies! They're all collecting in the waiting room! Uncle James never kept them waiting. He said they'd tear the place apart or set fire to it or both if he kept them waiting."

"Good God!" Phillips said. He seemed genuinely appalled; at his forgetfulness or the prospect of taking the clinic, Lilian wondered. She pressed the point.

"There's no one left to take it except you," she said. "Shall I put out the things or give them their cards?"

He looked at her curiously.

"You aren't afraid of them?" he asked her.

"Of *them*? Heavens, no! I know all about *them*."

It was a complete answer, saying much more than those simple words and Dr Phillips had the wit to understand her. A girl to be reckoned with. A girl to put down? Later, yes. Until after the inquest, unfortunately no.

Lilian gathered together the cards of all those she knew would be attending, while Dr Phillips quickly prepared his late partner's surgery for the invasion. Lilian's appearance in the noisy waiting room produced an instant hush. Mrs Gladstone was on her feet whispering her relief and her shock over Dr Williams. Yes, the ambulance men had told her. The questions were beginning again in louder and louder aggrieved voices when Dr Phillips appeared and shouted an order for silence.

He was obeyed. He explained in short sharp sentences that Dr Williams had died suddenly that afternoon. In view of the urgency of their needs he would attend to them. But it was for the last time. There would be no further clinics at this surgery. He was alone now in the practice. He could not undertake the work. They must all transfer to another doctor. Did they understand?

132

They understood but they were too shocked to speak. They got up one by one and shambled off to the familiar room for the last time, staring into a black future where they would have to make incredible efforts to secure the relief they must have.

As soon as she saw that everything was in order Lilian left the annexe. Though she wanted to secure the papers from her uncle's room she dared not go upstairs until Dr Phillips had left the surgery and she was alone in the house. So she went instead to the kitchen and having got there, discovered that she was very hungry. A sandwich lunch in the dinghy and a hurried tea at Hamble hardly made up for a missed breakfast. It was now after nine in the evening and she was starving. In the fridge were the lamb chops she had provided for supper for Uncle James and herself. She grilled them with tomatoes and mushrooms and ate the lot.

When she had cleared away and washed up it was nearly eleven. The house was very quiet, the whole of the waiting room in darkness. Should she go upstairs now or leave it until the next day when she would insist upon seeing the police and could have their protection while she made her search? But suppose one of them, Phillips or Waters or even that Southampton pair, Armitage and Thompson, knew what Uncle James had done, knew that it proved their hold over him, knew that the other papers exposed them? Suppose they meant to destroy this evidence and came in the night?

She was working herself up into another panic. She took hold of herself with a great effort. Things had gone on in this house, in this practice, that were outside the proper conduct of medicine, but even those that had been criminal a few years ago were now within the law. She had no excuse for falling into nightmares and melodrama. She had only to behave naturally and tell all she knew to the police and the solicitors as soon as she could safely do so. Surely there could be no danger in that plan, though there might be some delay.

She went upstairs at once, determined to secure whatever Uncle James had meant her to find. His bedroom door was unlocked, nothing inside seemed to have been moved. As usual there were a few clothes lying about, a jacket and trousers half on, half off a small chair, creased and crumpled as they always looked when he wore them. She went straight to the chest of drawers, unlocked the bottom drawer as directed and found there a small parcel addressed to herself. As she closed the drawer again, undecided whether to lock it or not she heard a step on the stair.

She had left the bedroom door open from a vague superstitious fear of shutting herself into the room of a dead man. So whoever it was would be guided by the light and come straight to this room. She snatched up the discarded suit, draping it over her left arm and the hand that held the parcel. With the other hand she pulled her own bedroom key from round her neck, moved silently out to the landing and leaned over the bannisters.

"Who is it?" she called down.

"It's me, Gladdy," a familiar voice answered.

It was indeed the stout daily, pausing for breath on the landing below. Before Lilian could ask the obvious question Mrs Gladstone gave the answer.

"Dr Phillips just come to my house, seeing I'd gone home after the surgery. 'She's there all alone in the place,' he said. 'I can't ask her over to mine,' he said. 'Seeing as how I'm a bachelor. But she didn't ought to be alone,' So naturally I offered to come up myself."

"That's very sweet of you," Lilian said steadily. "But I'm all right. It was a great shock, of course, but we all know it wasn't unexpected. Not altogether, was it?"

Mrs Gladstone had by this time arrived on the top landing. She was carrying a zipper bag which she put down beside her while she got her breath. Lilian stared at the bag. Mrs Gladstone smiled.

"I told him," she said, "and he quite agreed. 'You stay with her,' he said, 'as long as she needs you. We can't have her left all alone in that big house with a cold corpse for company.' "

Mrs Gladstone was enjoying herself. Lilian said coldly, "My uncle's body was taken to the mortuary some hours ago, Gladdy. So there is really nothing for you to stay for."

"I didn't expect ingratitude," Mrs Gladstone said, her voice hardening. "In a time of sorrow, too. But it's what we have to expect these days. No feeling. No gratitude."

"Please, please," Lilian said. "You mustn't take it like that, Gladdy. It's just that I don't want to impose on you. I do appreciate your kindness in coming, but . . ."

"You don't want me here. So how do I get home to-night? The buses is off by now."

"I'll run you back in the car."

"Dr Phillips locked Dr Williams' garage and took the key. For safety's sake, he said."

Safety! Whose safety? Lilian fought down her fear, managed a short laugh.

"Then you must stay, of course. I'm sorry you should have all this trouble. I'll put you in the end room here."

Still with the suit over her arm but slipping her room key into the hand that held the parcel under the hanging jacket, she let Mrs Gladstone into the end room. It was the spare room; it had held no visitor since Aunt Emily died.

"You know where to find sheets and pillow cases, don't you?" she said briskly. "On the airing cupboard round the boiler. If you'll just fetch some I'll get rid of these things and help you make the bed."

Mrs Gladstone did not look very pleased with this suggestion, but she could not refuse it. While she was downstairs Lilian unlocked her room door, put the parcel in her own desk, locked the latter, folded the clothes and put them back tidily on the bed in Uncle James's room, where Mrs Gladstone found her when she came back with the linen. By this time Lilian had emptied two drawers of the chest and the suit was flanked by piles of shirts and underclothes.

"I think I'll ask the Red Cross to dispose of these," she said when Mrs Gladstone appeared. "Don't you think that would be a good idea?"

135

Mrs Gladstone did not reply. She spoke very little as Lilian helped her to make the bed. She accepted an offer to make herself a cup of tea or cocoa if she preferred that. She had not come up again from the kitchen when Lilian, having carefully locked her own room door went down to her bath. But there was a light under Mrs Gladstone's door when the girl returned to the top landing.

"Goodnight, Gladdy," she called, to cover the noise of her key in the lock. A faint voice answered.

Lilian had a portable radio in her room. She put it on for the late news summary. She heard that two bodies had been washed ashore in Lyme Bay but she was not impressed. People were always getting drowned off our shores in the summer season. Well, all the year round, really.

Chapter 14

In the middle of the night Lilian woke suddenly. There was a scraping sound at her door. She switched on her bedside light and at that moment her door key fell out on to the floor. It slid as it reached the carpet. *Slid!*

Lilian bounded out of bed and flung herself on the key, just in time. The paper on which it had fallen disappeared rapidly under the door. Evidently her putting on a light had momentarily halted whoever it was outside had attemped, by securing her key, to open her door. Whoever? Mrs Gladstone, of course. Mrs G., under orders from Dr Phillips, who had locked up her uncle's car to prevent her taking the daily home. Perhaps, which was more important, to prevent her leaving Azalea Road during the night.

For some time Lilian struggled to make sense of these manoeuvres. Dr Phillips must imagine she knew more than was really the case of the facts of the irregularities in the practice. Otherwise surely what he was doing would only give her ideas, would only confirm suspicions. He might embarrass, even block, her movements outside the house, but he could not set about anything serious until after the inquest on Uncle James and the subsequent funeral.

After a period of near panic, in which she almost decided to run away to the police on foot, she decided to wait until the morning and the arrival of an officer to interview her. It needed a great effort to lie still, waiting for the slow night to pass, but her youth helped her. She was very tired, she had not been sleeping soundly or she would have lost her key. More settled in her mind now, with the key secure under her pillow, she soon fell soundly to sleep and did not wake up until Mrs Gladstone thumped on her door, calling loudly, "Miss Lilian! It's half-past nine, Miss Lilian! Shall I bring your breakfast up to you?"

She roused herself with an effort, all the fears and griefs and perplexities of the night before crowding back into her mind. She managed to sit up, to answer, "No, thank you. I'll be down in five minutes." She slipped out of bed to go softly to the door and listen. Yes, Mrs Gladstone was walking back downstairs. Presently a door banged below. Mrs Gladstone was in one of her tempers.

Lilian put on slacks and an ample sweater that hid bulging pockets. With the keys round her neck as before and the diaries, which were small but fat, in her pockets, she left her room, drawing a deep breath of relief to find the landing deserted. She could almost laugh now to remember how she had shrunk from unlocking her door, imagining Mrs Gladstone or even Dr Phillips standing outside to take the key from her before she could use it again, dragging it from the ribbon round her neck, perhaps dragging the ribbon tight—

In that sudden terror she had remembered how as a child of thirteen she had used her window ledge to make her way along the house, first to the bathroom ledge, then to her uncle and aunt's bedroom. It had been quite easy then, she was taller and stronger now, though perhaps no longer so fearless. But she had hesitated. If 'they' knew she had left her room by the window, that would instantly prompt 'them' to put a ladder to it and get in from outside. So the diaries must go with her everywhere until she could lodge them with Uncle James's solicitor. But she would lock her room up at all times or they would guess she had not left anything of interest there.

Since it was Sunday there was no work in the annexe. There were no telephone calls either, which surprised Lilian until she learned from Mrs Gladstone that Dr Phillips had had the number transferred to his own house.

"Suppose someone wants to ring *me* up?" Lilian asked indignantly.

"Dr Phillips would put you through, of course," said Mrs Gladstone.

"I see. Well, at any rate I can make calls myself."

"I don't know so much. He said you wasn't in a fit state to go anywheres or speak to anyone. Shock, he said. You

138

don't know what you look like, Miss Lilian. Downright ill, believe me."

It was said in the kind, homely way Lilian had always liked in Mrs Gladstone. She *couldn't* be an enemy. She couldn't *really* have wanted to make her way into her bedroom last night. Or could she?

"I've put the fire on in the study," Mrs Gladstone said. "You've got to see that police officer this morning, haven't you? He's due about eleven, the doctor said. You go and wait for him. I'll just run up and make your bed."

"I've made it," Lilian said, calmly." But you can go up and take off the sheets on your bed and put them in the laundry basket. I hope you slept well, by the way. I should have asked you sooner."

"As well as could be expected in a strange house," Mrs Gladstone said, with anger in her voice. "But I'm staying till the funeral, doctor said."

"Dr Phillips is not the master of this house," Lilian answered, anger swamping caution. "He has no right to order, to ask you, to stay here without consulting me."

"Being a doctor he's every right to do what he considers best for you in your present state."

"Dr Phillips is not my doctor. He has no possible right to attempt to treat me for ... for ... I haven't consulted him and I don't mean to."

"There's the front bell now," Mrs Gladstone said, disregarding Lilian's outburst. "That'll be him, I expect."

If she meant Dr Phillips she was probably wrong, Lilian thought. The doctor never used their front door,—*her* front door now. He walked in and out as he pleased from the annexe. No. The new caller would be the police, to take her statement.

She was right. From just outside the study where she had held her recent conversation with Mrs Gladstone she heard the caller announce himself as Detective-inspector Clark to see Miss Bartlett. She had just time to move across to the fire and face about before Mrs Gladstone showed him in, pronouncing his name and rank in satisfied tones.

Now she'll ring up Phillips and he'll be over in less than

five minutes to stop me giving anything away about the practice, she told herself as she greeted the newcomer and offered him a seat, before sitting down herself in her late uncle's armchair.

"It was someone else who came yesterday evening and saw my uncle," she said.

Detective-inspector Clark was fishing in the pocket of his mackintosh for a notebook. His head was lowered, his voice rather gruff as he answered, "Yes, Miss Bartlett. He understood you were suffering from shock."

"I wasn't actually," Lilian answered, "but Dr Phillips didn't want me to speak to the police."

"Why was that?"

Don't rush it, she told herself. She tried to remember if Uncle James had ever had a plain clothes detective on the premises, but could only remember uniformed men with helmets under their arms, escorting drunks, carrying in sick children from the street outside, inquiring about named patients.

"I suppose he thought I *ought* to be suffereing from shock."

"But he was wrong?"

"Not altogether. But I wasn't as surprised as I would have been if Uncle James . . ."

"Did you expect something of this sort to happen?"

"Yes."

"You thought it was possible he might commit suicide?"

"Or have a sudden heart attack," she said cautiously.

"There was a note for you. When you saw it did you jump to the right conclusion?"

This was an odd way for a police officer to put a question. Lilian, who had been on the verge of explaining the apparent falseness of the note, merely nodded.

"The note told you it was suicide?"

"Yes."

The note told her that, but not Uncle James. The look of satisfaction that spread over the detective's face built up her caution still further. She would tell her story but confide nothing at this stage. Better to wait for the inquest.

So she described exactly how she had found her uncle
and how Dr Phillips had come in to take complete com-
mand of the situation.

"And relieve you of doing anything yourself. That must
have been a great comfort to you."

"Yes. But I have run the house for my uncle since my
aunt died. I could probably have coped. I look after the
secretarial side of the practice."

"Dr Phillips has told me about your devoted work for
the patients."

Again, how unlike any policeman she had ever met,
Lilian decided. But she simply got up and said, "As I
wasn't here I don't know what Dr Phillips told you about
the practice. My uncle kept the notes of his private patients
in here, but the National Health files are all in my office."

"Dr Phillips said he would not touch any of his partner's private papers, but he took away the practice files."

"I see. Was it Dr Phillips then who locked the door of
this room last night? I thought it had been you or rather
the officer who came last night—in uniform," she added.

"I thought you didn't see him?"

"I didn't speak to him. I was upstairs. I saw him from
a window as he left the house. But about this room. Mrs
Gladstone was able to open the door this morning because
she told me she had put the fire on. That was just before
you arrived."

She moved to the window and looked out.

"Is that your car?" she asked.

It was the only one in the road outside the house. It
had no distinguishing mark.

"It is," Detective-inspector Clark told her. "My own.
It's Sunday, isn't it? I drove from my own home on
instructions. To hear your account of finding your uncle
dead."

There was silence between them. At last Lilian said, "Is
there anything else you want to ask me?"

"No. I don't think so. Is there anything else you want
to tell me?"

"No. I don't think so."

Whoever the man Clark was, Lilian decided, he did not

invite confidence. Quite the opposite. The earnest young man in uniform she had watched taking leave of Dr Phillips on the steps of the house the night before, settling his helmet on his head before stepping astride his motor scooter and pushing off, yes, that young man would have encouraged her to tell him her thoughts about the suicide note, about the diaries, about Uncle James's miserable bondage in a bent set-up, a crooked practice, a concern devoted to money-making in any way available, medical or not. But she would say nothing of this to Mr Clark, detective or not. She led the way to the door of the study and saw him leave, polite, baffled, but able to reassure her about the probability of an uneventful inquest.

"That's all *you* know," Lilian told herself, going back to the study.

Should she ring up the local police station to ask for the bona fides of their Detective-inspector Clark? No, because Dr Phillips was still in control of the telephone. It was switched to internal calls only and she would need an outside line. She could not get this because her office was locked.

And why had Phillips left her alone with Clark? Was she meant to confide? Was she being given an opportunity to pour out all her fears, her suspicions; produce the material she must be hiding, with her new craze for locking the dead man's desk, locking up his bottom drawer in his room, locking her own door whether she was in or out? Yes, she had been given the opportunity and she had not taken it. Because she had nothing to tell or because she was too cagey?

Lilian felt more cheerful, more confident after she had got rid of Mr Clark than at any time since Roy left London. She found an anorack in the hall cupboard, transferred the precious diaries to its deep inside pockets and calling out to Mrs Gladstone "I'm going out for my newspaper. They haven't sent it," she went quickly out of the front door and down the steps and along towards the shops.

She had gone about twenty yards when a motor scooter came buzzing along the road. On it rode a young police

142

officer in uniform and a helmet. He passed Lilian without looking at her, but she stopped, turned and watched his progress. He stopped outside 38 Azalea Road, walked up the steps and rang the bell. Lilian moved back until she was out of sight of the front door. She could see the young officer was speaking to someone in the house, Mrs Gladstone most likely. Should she run back, invite him in, explain about the other visit? Would that help or would it merely expose her to Phillips and his stooge, Mrs Gladstone? Better, surely, to leave matters as they were and see what happened. If Clark was not bogus, she would make a fool of herself by pouring out a tale of melodrama to the constable. If Clark was bogus, the constable's superiors would know a trick had been attempted. Or would they? Would Mrs Gladstone say there had been another police officer calling? Of course not. Only that she was out. Which was true.

She cursed her impulse to take action of some kind, however remote. She waited until the constable went back to his scooter. If he came her way she would stop him and take him back or explain a little and go on to the police station with him. But he rode off in the opposite direction, so Lilian walked on towards the newsagent's little shop on the next corner, always open on Sunday morning.

She bought her paper and some chocolates. She crossed the road to a public telephone and tried to ring up Roy, but he was out visiting patients, she was told. So she went home, deciding to wait until the next day before she attempted to get help in her predicament. On the next day she would visit Grant and Simmonds, Uncle James's named solicitors. They would tell her what to do and how to do it.

At lunch she asked Mrs Gladstone if anyone had rung her up or called to see her while she was out.

"No one at all," Mrs Gladstone answered. "Did you expect anyone?"

"Oh no," Lilian answered. "I just wondered."

She spent the rest of the day at home, reading Uncle James's diaries in her locked bedroom, going down for short chats with Mrs Gladstone, helping her with the meals, and later in the day sitting with her in the study watching television, while her thoughts strayed to her plans for the next day.

Dr Phillips did not appear at all. Nor was there any further communication from the police, not even a telephone call. She began to wonder if her doubts about Detective-inspector Clark were justified. But she comforted herself with the thought that Uncle James's solicitors, Grant and Simmonds, would advise her, tell her about his will, tell her what she ought to say at the inquest, tell her if she ought to go to the police about the note she had handed over to Dr Waters, who must have shown it to the coroner. Above all they must take into safe keeping those pathetic diaries, with their confession of weakness, of crazy, appalling mistakes, of failure, the degradation of blackmail, pitiless, ever continuing, from which he had not been able to escape. She promised herself a very careful, very complete retribution should fall upon the villains who had ruined him.

Dr Phillips held a morning surgery the next day at which Lilian attended, as usual, in her capacity of receptionist. When it was over the doctor went to her office.

"I hear the inquest is to be held tomorrow," he said. "In the afternoon, to suit my convenience, which is considerate of them. I will drive you there. You realise you will have to give evidence as you were the first to see the body and you found the suicide note."

"Yes," she answered, but added, "The detective who saw me yesterday might have told me about the inquest, I think."

"Probably didn't know himself until later."

Lilian left it at that. But she said after a few seconds silence, "I take it the phone here is now back to normal. With Mrs Gladstone staying and me here too."

"Yes, yes." He did not seem to want to discuss it.

"I may want to ring up my friends," Lilian went on. "It will seem rather strange to them that I did not do so yesterday."

"What friends?" he asked sharply.

Lilian stared. His arrogant impertinence sent a wave of

144

anger through her, but she held it back. With the transfer of responsibility so near she could afford to treat this lightly.

"Just friends," she said, with a forced laugh. "There's a brother of Aunt Emily's too that ought to be told, but I think he's abroad. Poor Uncle James had no relations of his own living. That I know of," she added, wondering if Grant and Simmonds might even produce a distant cousin or two who would help her.

Dr Phillips gave her another sharp look but went away, without any more questions. She rang up an old college friend, hoping he was listening in at the phone in his surgery. When she heard his car leave the annexe park a few minutes later she was sure she had been right in this.

Messers Grant and Simmonds had their offices on the second floor of a dingy building in a part of Holborn that had so far escaped redevelopment. The brass plate beside the stone staircase at the entrance was tarnished, the letters, in a florid Victorian style, looked very worn. Lilian stopped to stare at them, wondering for the first time how long Uncle James had used this firm, how long ago he had made the will he referred to in his letter.

She found the offices less dingy than the brass plate suggested. In fact the waiting room into which she was shown had modern chairs and a table, bare walls, no shelves of dusty red-taped rolls of deeds, but a selection of fairly recent magazines.

"I have no appointment, but I want to see Mr Grant," Lilian had told the young man with heavy side-burns in the outer office. He had stared at her and explained that there had been no Mr Grant in the office for a very long time. Nor a Mr Simmonds either. The present partners were Mr Ferguson, who was expected back from lunch any time now, and Mr Long, who had gone into the country to see a client.

"Then I would like to see Mr Ferguson," Lilian told the youth.

"What name, please?"

"Miss Bartlett. I am a niece of—of a former client, Dr Williams, Dr James Williams."

The youth showed her into the waiting room and went away, leaving the door partly open. Lilian looked at her watch. Three o'clock. She hoped the solicitor would not linger over his lunch. Three o'clock was the usual time to begin work again in business, she had been told.

Very soon there was a step on the stairs, slow, deliberate, accompanied by heavy breathing. But when a voice rang out, calling for Cyril, cursing Cyril for a lazy bastard, she sprang to her feet, slipping behind the half-open door, terrified, despairing. The voice was unmistakable. She had heard it for over an hour yesterday morning. The voice of so-called Detective-inspector Clark of the Metropolitan police.

There was a mirror on the waiting room wall. It reflected a small part of the corridor outside. Lilian saw the young man called Cyril come into it, sulky, indignant, muttering "Can't be everywhere at once, Mr Ferguson, can I? I mean to say..."

She dived back behind the door. When she peeped out again at the mirror she saw an unmistakable mackintosh, no hat this time, but the same grizzled hair framing the same bald patch. Uncle James's solicitor was as bent as his partner, was in the same racket, whatever that might be, was no secure help and prop, was the enemy she had rightly suspected.

She heard the pair go into another room and shut the door. The stupid boy had not yet announced her. In any case Ferguson would not see her, knowing she would recognise him. She thought of the diaries in the large satchel she was carrying and knew she had no time to lose.

Creeping out of the room and along the corridor she was nearly paralysed with fear that the pair might suddenly pounce on her. But she gained the outer door, passed it silently, ran swiftly down the stairs and out into the street.

There was a taxi in a small rank quite close, but she did not take it. Instead she walked rapidly to the Underground station, and took a ticket to South Kensington.

Chapter 15

Lilian left South Kensington Underground station in a mood that was chiefly defiant but held a distinct background of panic. Betrayal had been altogether too evident in the last forty-eight hours. Uncle James's death had brought it to the surface, but she realised now that her whole life for an incalculable time had been a dangerously shaky footing over an evil, foetid swamp of deception and crime. With Uncle James's death the surface had cracked, at least as far as she herself was concerned. Her feet had gone through into the ooze, she had understood far more than was safe, swift measures had been taken to prevent her finding out any more. Even now, she thought, hurrying through the arcade outside the station entrance, she was probably being pursued, because she could not hope that the gormless Cyril at the office of Grant and Simmonds would have forgotten her name.

She looked about her for a public telephone box. Not to attempt a call. She had avoided that when she left Holborn, but because she had forgotten the number of Sir Henry Killick's house in the Kensington Square whose name she had fortunately remembered. The delay was dangerous, but as she looked about her before entering the box, she was comforted by the presence of a great many people going to and fro. She might be accosted, but surely not robbed or kidnapped.

Her search was quickly made and she was very soon on her way again, walking quickly, her satchel held tightly under her arm, with the strap wound twice round her wrist. She had considered taking a taxi, but again discarded it because it meant waiting and signalling or going in the wrong direction to the nearest rank. Besides, the square where the Killicks lived was not more than ten minutes walk away. She marched along briskly, her confidence growing as she neared her goal.

Until she turned into the square, checked the numbers of the houses near her, looked across the central garden at the house she sought, which she now recognised. And saw, with a chill at her heart, a small knot of untidily dressed, mop-haired youths standing near the pillared steps, apparently in conference and unmistakably waiting.

It was ridiculous, she told herself, to imagine they had anything to do with her, but nevertheless she began to think frantically of a way of coming to the house that would give them less notice of her arrival than walking half the length of that side of the square. Unfortunately the Killicks lived very nearly at the centre of one of the longer sides. She was now standing on the one opposite.

She looked at the central garden. There was a gate just in front of where she stood, so presumably there would be another on the opposite side. Keeping herself hidden from the group of waiting youths she found this was so, but her plan for moving unseen through the garden, hiding behind bushes or persuading those who were exercising children or dogs to see her across to the door of the house in safety, was defeated. The gate was locked and padlocked, so presumably the one on the other side was equally secure. There was no one at all in the garden. It was well kept, obviously in use, but on this damp, cold, autumn afternoon evidently no one wanted to loiter there.

So the only thing to do was to walk round the square on the narrow footpath behind the parked cars and then to make a dash across the road when she was opposite the Killick's house. Not a violent dash, she told herself severely as the moment approached. Just a swift movement, if the traffic permitted, up the steps and ring the bell and turn to meet any opposition that dared to assail her. If only there was a traffic warden about. But naturally on this occasion, this first occasion she had ever wished to find one hovering round his charges, the uniform was absent. No warden, no nursemaid or au pair girl, no young mother, not even a shopper or an elderly person taking a constitutional. At nearly four in the afternoon? What a hope!

The group she feared had not moved away, she found, when she turned the second corner and was barely twenty yards from them. They were watching the wide pavement on the other side of the road. So far her approach was successful. With a dry mouth and a pounding heart she stepped out from the protecting screen of a large car and walked very quickly across the road.

In her excitement she had forgotten to look for traffic. A taxi was bearing down on her, the screech of its brakes brought all heads in her direction. The driver, recovering, leaned out to curse her, but the youths poured round him on each side and at the bottom of the steps Lilian found two of them blocking her path.

One, lowering at her from a heavily beared face, she did not know. But the other she recognised. One of Uncle James's junkies. One of the most insistent, the worst addicted of the hard type junkies. She had seen him biting his nails, whimpering, degraded, disgusting, before he got his fix. And afterwards a little king, proud, confident and to her equally if not more disgusting.

"Barry!" she said now, in the voice he must remember. "Fancy seeing you here! Have you got yourself another doctor since poor Dr Williams died?"

His mouth dropped open. He had not thought he would be recognised. The others who were closing in behind stood still. They were interested. Their empty minds and poor enfeebled brains were easily carried away by a new situation. Concentration had long ago become impossible.

In the pause that followed, short as it was, Lilian had time to see that the way behind her up the steps to the front door was blocked, but to her right there was a gap in the railings with a little open gate at the top of a steep flight of steps leading down to an area door.

It presented her only chance of escape from a scuffle, the object of which she guessed was to snatch her satchel with its precious contents. Dr Phillips must have organised this, but how did he *know*? He knew everything. It was hopeless.

She had a moment of paralysis, a despairing wish to

give up the struggle. But she heard her own voice repeating the standard phrases of the surgery receptionist to the still shaken youth before her and the crowded faces behind him.

A touch on her arm together with a growl from his bearded companion broke her inaction. She shot forward so violently that the junkie, pushed off balance, fell back against his friends. She was down the area steps before the confusion behind her released a pursuit. The area door was open. She rushed inside. The door was instantly pushed shut, locked and bolted.

Lilian found herself, to her surprise, in a fairly large, comfortably furnished room where she had expected the kitchen premises, perhaps an outer scullery or laundry room, belonging to the Killicks. Her astonishment and her misgivings were renewed when the young woman who had shut the door and who had presumably opened it to receive her, said quietly, "Well, Miss Bartlett, here you are."

Lilian sank into a chair. Another trap, another betrayal, or what? But at least her antagonist this time was a girl of about her own age and not at all frightening to look at, so she said, defiantly, "What do you mean by that and anyway who the hell are you?"

"She's my sister," a man's voice behind Lilian said. "She's looking after me at present. Dr Cartwright found us the flat."

"Dr . . . *Roy* !"

"That's right."

The face was familiar, but rounder, healthier, smiling.

"You're Giles Long," Lilian said. "I sent your letter on to Roy."

The young man nodded.

"He got me into this flat with Kay to look after me. Well away from . . . Well, Dr Williams and all that."

"My Uncle is dead," Lilian told him. "The clinic folded the day after."

"So all those bums up in the road. Was I scared! I thought they'd come for me." He stared at Lilian. "Had they come for *you*?"

"In a way, yes. Look, Giles. I can't tell you now but I will later if I can. Just now I'm trying to contact Sir Henry Killick. How do I get upstairs to his part of the house?"

The pair shook their heads.

"You can't," Kay said. "We're a self-contained flat. It's a furnished flat, rent by the week, month's notice and all that jazz."

Lilian's spirits sank again.

"Then how do I get to the front door? Up by the way I came down?"

" 'Fraid so."

But Giles had gone to the barred window and looked out.

"I think they've faded," he said. "I heard a whistle from the end of the road just as you arrived. Copper on the beat. Probably thought there was a fight on."

"It might have looked like that," Lilian said, smugly. "I did push one of them out of my way."

"Good for you," said Giles, smiling. He went to the door. "I'll check. Stand by for sudden retreat."

But none was necessary. The pavement, the road, the square were empty of any ragged, long-haired figures. Giles beckoned to Lilian, escorted her up the steps of the area, watched her approach the front door of the house, ring the bell, be admitted. Then he went back to the basement flat.

"I'd better ring up," he said. "The question is, which?"

"What d'you mean?" His sister was puzzled.

"Dr Cartwright said ring him if I came to know Miss Bartlett was in any sort of jam. Well, she is. Dr Phillips said report to him if I found Miss Bartlett was in touch with Killick or Cartwright. Well, now she's certainly in touch with Killick. Phillips said if I wasn't useful he'd get me thrown out of this new college I'm with."

"He mustn't do that!" Kay said in alarm.

"Besides, any hard news is worth ten quid a time, Phillips said. So what had I better do?"

"Ring them both," Kay told him. "How do we know

151

either bunch is really on the level?"

Meanwhile Lilian had been shown into a room on the ground floor of the house by the parlourmaid who remembered both her face and her name.

"Is Sir Henry expecting you, miss?" she asked, looking with controlled disapproval at Lilian's dishevelled appearance.

"No. No, I'm afraid not," the girl answered. Never explain, Aunt Emily had taught her. Unless to a friend or unless it can't be helped. Times had changed, but perhaps Aunt Emily was still right in this respect.

"Is he out?" she asked, blushing when she remembered that her first question had been to discover if he was at home. The maid had let her in, so of course he must be there.

"He is engaged, miss," the latter said severely. "But I will tell him you have called."

Lilian waited only ten minutes before Sir Henry appeared, striding across the room to shake her warmly by the hand.

"My dear Miss Bartlett," he said. "I do apologise for keeping you waiting. Come upstairs where there's a fire. I'm afraid Rachel is out for the day. She will be sorry to have missed you."

He had led her to the door and up the stairs while he was talking, going on smoothly in an even voice without any apparent hesitation or lack of material, as many of his fellow advocates, his adverse witnesses and the high court judges had often deplored.

The drawing room was empty but there was a cheerful log fire in the grate and one or two lamps already switched on to forestall the rapidly darkening sky.

Lilian, encouraged to tell her story and promised no interruption, began at the point where she had found her uncle's body and continued up to the discovery of Roy's former patient in the basement of the house and her final evasion of the junkies.

"What did they want? Any of them?" Sir Henry asked, when Lilian became silent at last.

"These, I think," she said, drawing out the diaries and handing them over.

"Ah."

It was a sound of great satisfaction, but the barrister only flapped over a page or two to verify that they were indeed Dr Williams's work and then laid them aside.

"This firm of solicitors, what was it—Grant and Simmonds?"

"Yes, but those aren't the names now. The clerk or whoever it was said there was a Mr Long and a Mr Ferguson. Mr Ferguson was the man who had pretended to be a detective-inspector. He called himself Clark."

"Did he see you at the office?"

"I don't know. I recognised his voice and his back in a mirror there was in the waiting room. I'm sure the clerk would tell him I wanted to see him about my uncle's will."

Sir Henry laughed suddenly.

"Bit of a shock for him, that. He must have thought— they must all have thought—you wouldn't know the name of your uncle's lawyer. That was why this Ferguson chap pretended to be a copper in order to get out of you, first, what you really thought of the suicide note—I wonder if Ferguson is the forger—and second what else you know about your uncle's private affairs?"

"I should think Dr Phillips must always have known more than I do."

"Perhaps he guessed there might be a written record but had never seen it."

She nodded.

"I think that must be it. Thank goodness I've been able to get it to a safe place."

Sir Henry smiled at her kindly.

"A temporary home for it," he said, smiling. "No, don't be afraid. But you see, private papers and wills and so on don't come my way except through solicitors who want me to speak for their clients. I can advise you, though. My advice is that you take your problems to a reliable solicitor of your own. I can give you a suitable name. Or better still, do you know, did you ever know, who your Aunt

Emily consulted?"

"No," Lilian answered sadly. "I was only fourteen when she died. I was away at school when it happened."

"I see. Then would you like me to suggest someone?"

"Yes. I would very much. But I think Dr Phillips would somehow stop me going to see him. And the diaries..."

Sir Henry looked at his watch.

"I'll see if I can get..." He left the room and came back in a very short time.

"A friend of mine called Bourke," he said. "He's interested and he agreed to come here directly and take your instructions."

"That sounds very important," Lilian said, smiling for the first time since Sir Henry had begun to question her story. "I'm much more used to taking instructions than giving them."

"Far too much," Sir Henry said. "Don't let young Roy bully you, will you?"

"Roy!" She had almost forgotten Roy.

"Yes, Roy. You'll have to attend the inquest on your uncle. Roy will be there. Be kind to him, won't you?"

The parlourmaid, appearing with tea and hot scones, saved Lilian from her fresh embarrassment. Very shortly afterwards Mr Bourke appeared and Sir Henry excused himself to attend a consultation in chambers, he said.

Mr Bourke, dark-haired, middle-aged, with a quiet firm voice, inspired immediate confidence in Lilian's confused mind and soothed her torn feelings to such an extent that she was able to give him a much more lucid account of her troubles and fears than she had to the more formidable barrister.

"I take it you have no wish to continue in your present job, even if they offer you a proper salary?" Mr Bourke asked, when she came to the end of her saga.

"I want to leave the house as soon as I possibly can," Lilian answered. "I know I have to stay in London for the inquest but afterwards..."

"Where will you go? To relations? To friends?"

"I have no near relations. Uncle James made it all

154

very difficult. You'll see from the diaries his first wife's relations and most of his early friends would have nothing to do with him when she died and he left his first practice to take on the one in Azalea Road. Then he married Aunt Emily and her relations disapproved of him, too. I know we never saw him or Aunt Emily when I was quite little and living with my own parents. I think Aunt Emily had a brother but I've never met him."

"The name would be ... ?" Mr Bourke asked, making another note on the sheet of paper he had been filling with the facts of Lilian's story.

She reddened.

"I don't know," she said. "I've been trying to remember. I wanted to write to him for help, but I couldn't remember."

"I expect I can find out," Mr Bourke told her quietly. "Now," he went on, "as I see it you must be very brave and very sensible. When you go home today Dr Phillips is almost certain to ask you where you've been and what you've been doing. Simply tell him you have visited friends and consulted your solicitor. I will give you my business address and the name of my firm. Tell him nothing else. Give him my name if he asks for it. You can tell him, too, that I shall be at the inquest, or represented there at any rate."

"Oh, will you really!" Lilian exclaimed, greatly relieved.

"My dear," Mr Bourke said with a fatherly smile. "These people you are up against are probably crooks, but not, I think, murderers."

"I think they've murdered Uncle James," Lilian said. "And perhaps poor Tom Markson. Ask Commander Hull."

"Who?"

"The very high-up policeman who's in charge of drug crimes, I think. Or immigrants. I don't know, really."

"I'll make it my business to find out," Mr Bourke said, adding Commander Hull to his notes.

"Will you take charge of the diaries for me?" Lilian asked.

"If you want me to. Let me see. I must give you a

155

receipt for them. I take it you have read them already and know the contents?"

"Oh yes," Lilian agreed sadly. "Poor Uncle James."

Her eyes filled with tears as she spoke. Mr Bourke slipped the diaries into his own case together with his notes. He checked once again Lilian's address and telephone number and then, getting up said, "And now I shall drive you home, young lady. You are not fit to take yourself there alone."

"But suppose they see you?"

"So much the better," said Mr Bourke belligerently. "So much the better."

Chapter 16

The inquest on Dr James Williams was opened in London on the same day that the resumed inquest on Dr Tom Markson was held in Southampton. Both inquiries were adjourned on requests from the police.

Roy had been summoned to attend in Southampton in case the coroner wished to repeat or question his former evidence as to the dates of his locum at Azalea Road and his acceptance of his present post. But no evidence of any kind was called. The whole business was over in less than half an hour. As Roy had insisted upon having the day off, apart from a few necessary visits, which he made early in the morning, he was able to take a fast train to London and appear at Dr Williams's inquest in the afternoon.

At Southampton West station, where he left his car, he saw Mr Markson on the platform. They travelled together, shared a taxi to the coroner's court and went in together to find seats in the public part of the hall.

Having secured two side by side, Roy left his to find Lilian among the waiting witnesses. He was almost afraid to see her in case his vision of her, that had grown considerably in beauty and charm during the intervening days since their last meeting, should prove to be false or dimmed by the trials and troubles she had suffered, according to his Uncle Harry.

For the barrister had rung him up at great length in the evening of the day on which she had battled her way to his house. He was full of admiration for her courage, her good sense and determination. But he told Roy she looked far from well and must, without alarming the crooks, be got away from Azalea Road as soon as her presence there was no longer needed by the law.

"I leave it to you, my boy," Uncle Harry had said, smoothly. "That is, if you're as serious about her as you appear to be. Otherwise it would be kinder to get out of the picture altogether."

Damn you for an interfering old so-and-so, Roy had thought, but he said, politely, "Won't she go to her relations for a bit?"

"There are none."

"Literally none? Not a single aunt, cousin or whatnot?"

"A vague uncle who is probably abroad, address unknown, occupation unknown, even name unknown at present, because she can't remember her Aunt Emily's maiden name. Lilian's solicitor, a friend of mine, Robert Bourke, should be able to discover this."

"I see. Well, thanks for the gen. I'll know how to go on."

Which was chiefly why he was here, in this coroner's court, looking for Lilian, afraid to find her, if Uncle Harry's description had been true, if the horrors and fears at Azalea Road had not destroyed her looks and her well-being, even if her courage had survived.

He need not have feared. When he did at last catch sight of her, talking rapidly in a low voice to a dark-haired man at her side, he was not only entranced by her resemblance to his cherished vision of her, but struck by instant jealousy at her apparently easy familiarity with the old man she was with. The long lost uncle? Or something far more sinister? He noticed Dr Phillips in the same row, a few seats further on and Mrs Gladstone, in an astonishing hat, just behind.

Lilian, looking up at the sound of his voice, blushed becomingly and introduced the stranger.

"Mr Bourke," she said, "who is very kindly here to— well, to look after me."

"My Uncle Harry knows you, I believe," Roy said, shaking hands.

"Indeed, yes," Mr Bourke answered and added, in a lower voice, "I suggest you meet us afterwards. These proceedings will be very short, I understand."

"Good," Roy answered. "Where?"

They agreed to go separately to Victoria Station, from

158

where Lilian would be taking a train home. They could find tea somewhere near there, Mr Bourke said vaguely. Roy suggested bringing Mr Markson along and Lilian agreed to that with some enthusiasm. Roy got back to his seat beside Tom's father just in time before the proceedings began.

As Mr Bourke had suggested they were very short. Lilian was called to identify her uncle and describe how she had found him dead, with a note addressed to her beside his hand. Dr Phillips, who had seen him a few minutes later rather reluctantly agreed under questioning by the coroner that the body was quite cold and in a state of rigor mortis, suggesting Dr Williams had died some hours before he was discovered. Dr Phillips said he had not seen his partner alive that day but he was in his usual state of health the day before.

Dr Waters told how he had been called by Dr Phillips, had confirmed the death, called for an ambulance for removal of the body, and notified the police after reading the note addressed to Miss Bartlett. Dr Waters gave a brief account of Dr Williams's general health. He had known him for many years and had been his regular doctor for the last ten.

The coroner called Mrs Gladstone to confirm the dead man's state of health on the day before his death and also the fact that though she usually went to the house on Saturday morning for the half day, Miss Lilian had told her she could give it a miss as she was taking the day off herself and leaving early, but would be back in time to attend to the evening clinic and give the doctor his supper afterwards. She agreed that she usually attended the clinic herself to keep order in the waiting room and that she had done so on that day and heard the sad news then.

The coroner announced that tests were being made to determine the exact cause and circumstances of the death, but were not yet completed. He adjourned the inquest for two weeks but issued a certificate for burial.

On the way out of the court Dr Phillips appeared just in front of Lilian and Mr Bourke. Roy had left by another door. The solicitor whispered to Lilian, "I think you should introduce me," so she moved forward and said, clearly, "Dr Phillips, I should like you to meet my lawyer, Mr Bourke."

Phillips stopped at once, and turned round. He was pale, stiffly controlled, but took the introduction calmly. While Mr Bourke, quiet and polite, explained briefly but quite openly how Miss Bartlett had come to consult him, he made no move.

"Miss Bartlett has already told me this," Dr Phillips said. "I take it you will advise her about the arrangements for the funeral. If she needs advice," he added, spitefully. "Miss Bartlett is not very easy to advise."

"I'm sure you would be the best person to suggest an undertaker," Mr Bourke said. "Doctors usually know of a reliable one in their own districts."

"That isn't very complimentary," Lilian could not help saying to stop herself giggling aloud. Dr Phillips gave her a furious look, but only said, "Miss Bartlett as acting secretary for her uncle knows as much as I do about our local undertakers."

He turned away, but was at once stopped by a constable, who said "Dr Phillips, sir, the coroner would like to have a word with you." There was no refusing this, so the doctor, more angry than ever, turned back into the building.

"That disposes of him while we find a cab," said Mr Bourke, leading the way to the taxi rank.

"Not to Victoria Station?" Lilian·asked. "What about . the others?"

"Tea at the new Scotland Yard," Mr Bourke told her. "Just along Victoria Street. The others know by now, too."

In a small room at Scotland Yard, with tea and biscuits on a tray, Lilian once more described the whole series of events from the time of her return home from Hamble with Dr Phillips to her first meeting with Mr Bourke.

"Does Phillips know you rumbled Ferguson?" Roy asked.

"I think he must know. He certainly knew I had gone

to see Sir Henry Killick. No one knew I had that letter from Uncle James. Not the forged suicide note; a letter giving me the names of Uncle James's solicitors, Grant and Simmonds. I wasn't altogether surprised to hear neither of these people was still in the firm, but Ferguson meant nothing to me, because he'd called himself Clark when he pretended to be a detective and was trying to find out how much I knew and whether I accepted the suicide note. It was only when I saw his back in the mirror in the waiting room and heard his voice I knew who he was and left the office at once."

"He wouldn't have wanted to see you anyway," Roy said. "I expect he'd ring up Phillips to get instructions."

"Dr Phillips is resourceful," said Mr Bourke drily. "I'm sure he would conclude that you had gone to Sir Henry and so he got in touch with the café or discothèque where he knew his junkie patients congregate and told them to stop you getting to the house. It wasn't a very good plan, very risky in fact from the point of view of the police getting wind of it. But it very nearly worked, didn't it?"

"But it did not, thanks to your young convert," said Mr Bourke, who had listened in silence and now turned to Roy with a smile.

"It was Uncle Harry's idea to let Giles Long have the flat with his sister when he left hospital," Roy said.

"He seems to be getting along fine," Lilian said, "I liked Kay Long. But Dr Phillips will get his hooks in again if he can, by blackmail if he can make that work."

"By roughing up if it doesn't," suggested Mr Markson. "Tom told me this sort of thing did happen. In that last letter I had from him. If only he had not tried to expose the whole thing. If only . . ."

"I think we shall find that he succeeded," said a new voice just behind them. Commander Hull drew up a chair and sat down. He bowed to Lilian and nodded to the others, including Mr Bourke, who obviously knew him quite well.

"The whole thing, Mr Markson," the Commander repeated gravely. "He had to take that last risk to prove what he suspected."

"A drug ring?" Lilian asked, turning a puzzled face to Hull. She was not surprised he had joined them. This whole strange meeting would be explained, she hoped. She went on, "I have thought for a long time Uncle James was giving far too much of the wretched stuff of all kinds. He wasn't really attempting treatment, just handing out supplies. But I'm sure he wasn't actually pushing it."

"The junkies themselves could push the surplus, couldn't they?" Roy suggested.

"Anyway, he really wasn't fit to know what he was doing these last few months," Lilian went on. "When Roy came and after that. I suppose they knew Tom had been drowned — the others, I mean. Uncle James *can't* have known and said or done *nothing*."

"He was under their thumbs," said Commander Hull, "or thought he was."

Lilian turned to him.

"You've read the diaries, then?"

"I've read the diaries."

She sighed her relief. Her last fear, her last doubt of 'the other side', as she had thought of Roy and his uncle and their friends, was now finally dispersed. She saw he was watching her closely. Did his doubts of *her* still persist? With all her heart she prayed this might not be so.

"I arranged for all of you to come here," said Commander Hull looking round the table, gathering their close attention, "to tell you something I must ask every one of you to keep absolutely secret at present. A press bulletin will be released, but it will not give the whole story. It relates to the bodies cast up in Lyme Bay. Two of the five have been identified positively. They were members of the crew of the liner *Antigone* which sailed again, short of five crew, two days after Dr Cartwright began his locum at Azalea Road. None of these bodies was wearing the shore going clothes belonging to them, nor were these clothes found on board the *Antigone* when their lockers

162

were checked before the ship sailed. It was assumed they had gone ashore in them and stayed ashore."

"Why were they drowned then?" Lilian asked.

"That is what everyone has been asking," said the Commander. "Why were they at sea? What in?"

"That idea about a raft?" Roy suggested.

"Quite. Those planks thrown up on the Chesil Beach. Do any of you know about that beach?"

All shook their heads.

"It lies on the west side of Portland, facing out across Lyme Bay. It is very steep to, which makes it extremely dangerous for bathing. No one except a really strong swimmer or a very foolhardy one attempts to do so. I think those five tried to land there on a crazy primitive raft, probably paddled, probably at night and came to grief. As they were intended to do."

His audience gasped or swore.

"Put off from some craft a little way off shore?" Roy suggested, when the first feeling of horror had subsided.

"Exactly. They must have been able to see the land quite close. Must have imagined it was a piece of cake, even on a flimsy raft with paddles."

"And when they were all in the water, struggling to swim in to land, the devils who took them there just sailed away and left them."

"Tom was there," Mr Markson said. He had gone very pale and spoke in a low breathless voice. "In that last letter. He told me he was going. He was not against the plan. But he would have seen. He would have understood the treachery, the murderous treachery to keep the game running, stop any loose talk, repeat the profit."

"Of what, for heaven's sake?" Lilian demanded.

"Illegal immigrants," Roy said. "But why like that? As crew members they only had to go on shore leave, get on a train for Birmingham . . ."

"Work vouchers," Mr Markson said. "Entry certificates. Which I know were supplied, forged in London, brought down by Dr Phillips, distributed by Dr Armitage in Overton. That's right, isn't it, Commander?"

Commander Hull nodded and then said to the others, "Mr Markson kindly watched the process in action with our assistance in the case of the *Iphigenia*. He recognised a medallion round the neck of a waiting patient at Armitage's surgery that he had noticed round the neck of a so-called crew member coming through the dock gates where Mr Markson was waiting with one of the local C.I.D. men.'

"I had gone to the surgery with the excuse of feeling ill after the adjournment of Tom's inquest," Mr Markson said. "I *was* ill. I very nearly went for Armitage in his room after I'd seen that medallion."

"I still don't understand," Lilian said. "Why all the complications? Why that charade at Hamble? The fishing boat and the launch and Roy watching through binoculars? And whatever it was Dr Armitage gave Dr Phillips."

"He gave him the particulars to go on the vouchers and so on," Commander Hull told her.

"But *why*? They were crew. Couldn't they just have gone to the surgery as they seem to have done and given those particulars at one consultation and collected the gen at the next?"

"No, Miss Bartlett. Because it was not all crew members who went on shore leave, though they were wearing the clothes of members of the crew. They were stowaways, who had made the journey in one of the holds of the ship."

So now she understood the whole scheme as the others had discovered it, or been told it, already. Stowaways travelled to Southampton in the hold with the knowledge and connivance of some of the regular crew, who fed them on the journey. Wearing their friends' clothes they went ashore, made their way to Dr Armitage's surgery, where they took their turn with the ordinary patients. They gave up their crew clothes and identification, put on roughly similar, but fresh clothes, received their forged papers and went off to the Midlands or wherever jobs had been arranged for them. But five of these illegal immigrants on *Antigone* had broken the rules, so carefully devised. They had got out of the dock area but had not gone at once to Dr Armitage. Instead they had taken trains going north, to join relatives who had urged them to come, giving addresses where they could be found. This meant that five of the crew were hiding on their own ship below, waiting for their borrowed clothes and papers to be brought back to them. They found they had been cheated, there was nothing for them.

"How were the clothes and things brought back?" Lilian asked when she had thought this over.

"We're not absolutely certain. Probably that old fishing boat nosing alongside among other supply ships or work-ships and passed through an empty porthole."

"They were pretty dim not to go to their bo'sun or whoever and simply say what had happened. They'd have their shore leave cut, but I imagine the officers of that ship had a shrewd idea what was on," Roy said.

"Yes, silly chumps," Mr Markson agreed. "But you don't realise the general fear of authority, dread of the boss, terror of punishment those poor devils feel in their own country. Rather more now than in the days of the Raj, because the law in those days was less corrupt, fairer the higher up you went. Those seamen simply wouldn't dare to expose themselves to their captain. They'd expect to be sacked, whereas actually the blind eye would be turned to avoid any possible delay in sailing."

"Didn't the disappearance of the five delay sailing?"

"Only for twelve hours, one tide," Commander Hull said. "They were being searched for all that time in the pubs and so on. It was after *Antigone* sailed the search was extended to the Midlands and the North."

With this statement Commander Hull broke up the meeting, refusing to answer any more questions or give any more information.

Mr Markson went off on his own, as did Mr Bourke. But before the latter left he drew Roy away from the table where Lilian still sat waiting for a final word with the Commander.

"Dr Cartwright," Mr Bourke said, with a very serious look at the young man, "You must not think me impertinent, if I ask whether your friendship with Miss Bartlett is casual, in the nature of an acquaintenceship or something more substantial."

"Hardly that," Roy said, trying not to laugh. "You make it sound like suet pudding. At present it's more like . . . like . . ."

"Candyfloss?"

"God, no. Like—Oh hell, not food anyway. I'm in love with her—I think."

"Yes." Mr Bourke's face softened a little. "My problem, as her legal adviser, is this. She has no relations as far as I've got at present. She has no means, until we find her uncle's will if such exists. Her late aunt's will can be consulted, of course. I have put that in hand. She will have to stay in London until after the funeral and she will have to attend and given evidence at the resumed inquest in two weeks time. But there will be at least a week's interval between those dates and I wish very much she could spend it away from Azalea Road. Matters there are coming to a head as we all realise now, I think. Is your friendship—are your relations with Miss Bartlett far enough advanced for her to get an invitation to stay with, for instance, your parents?"

"I don't know," Roy said.

He knew what he intended, but he was not going to be ordered about by old man Bourke, friend of Uncle Harry, legal adviser to Lilian, nosey parker in chief. But the solicitor was still waiting for an answer.

"I'll arrange something," Roy said vaguely," if you think it's all that important."

"I think it is not only important, but urgent," Mr Bourke said as he turned away.

So Roy had just time to say to Lilian, between kisses, in the taxi that took them along Victoria Street to the station, "Look, darling, I'm not going to be able to get away again for weeks. After the funeral, can't you come down to me for a bit? I'm sure the Pratts could put you up."

166

"Aren't they living in Dr Armitage's house?"

"Separate flat. Own front door. No connection. Great friends of Nancy and George Mellish."

"I know. Rather in the lions' mouth, though, wouldn't it be?"

"Possibly Nance could have you as well as me. I don't suppose she'd mind us sharing my place."

"Try the Pratts then," Lilian said. She was no prude, but she didn't intend to be rushed.

At Azalea Road the house was in darkness and very cold. Mrs Gladstone had gone, with all her possessions, leaving her bedroom in disorder. She had, however, left a note to say she would call in the morning for her wages, but was leaving at once as she had found a more convenient post nearer her home.

Lilian switched on the fire in the study and went to her office. The small room was quite empty. No table, no chair, no filing cabinet, no telephone switchboard. In the study, however, the telephone was in working order. She checked with exchange that the line was a simple outside link. The operator did not know when the alterations had been made. But of course Mrs Gladstone must have seen it through.

Having sorted out this question, Lilian went to the door that led into the annexe. It was locked, but the key no longer hung on the hook beside it. However, the Yale lock, used at night, was still in place on her side. She released the catch and fixed it in the locked position. She also drew across an ancient rather rusty chain that ran in a groove at hand level. Feeling doubly secure she went to the kitchen. Mrs Gladstone had left her half a loaf, a pat of butter, two eggs, a banana and a small piece of dry cheese. The rest had gone, except for a few tins that Lilian always kept at hand for emergencies.

She scrambled the eggs, made herself some coffee and took this simple meal on a tray to the study, where she ate it by the glowing electric fire, wondering a little what Dr Phillips intended to do with the practice, but glad to leave

167

her cares to her new-found uncle-substitute, Mr Bourke, while she let her dreams range in happy freedom over a life of blissful happiness with Roy.

So far away from reality had her dreams carried her that she did not hear the sounds of the front door opening, footsteps in the hall, the turn of the handle of the study door. She did not understand what was happening until she found herself surrounded by three figures, grotesquely disguised by stocking masks. A hand cut off her scream of terror, more hands held her, seized and bared her flailing arms. She scarcely felt the expert prick of the needle, but she knew she was helpless and feared her death. A wall of blackness engulfed her and her fear.

Chapter 17

Lilian woke first in darkness, with a thick head and a very dry mouth. She found she was in bed, concluded it was her own, but was too dazed to investigate. She merely turned on her side and slept again.

The second time she woke her brain was clear, but her head ached abominably, her thirst was worse than ever. She was no longer confused however, she remembered quite clearly what had happened to her. Lifting herself on one elbow, she looked about.

She was in bed, wearing her own underclothes, with the rest of her garments hung neatly over a chair under a window. The room was small, sparely but pleasantly furnished and perfectly clean. Chintz curtains covered the window through which daylight gave the muted view she had of her surroundings.

Rather shakily she got out of bed, first tried the door, which she found locked as she expected, then went to the window and pulled the curtains. There were bars across the frame, not put there recently and quite firm. They did not prevent her pushing open the latched half pane, but there was no possibility whatever of climbing out.

Below there was a garden, well kept, though untidy now with fallen leaves and decaying withered stems of herbaceous plants in the borders. Her watch, which she was thankful to find on her wrist, had stopped, but responded to winding. She set it at random and beginning to feel cold, dressed and added the top coat she found laid over the foot of the bed. Then she went back to the window.

The view beyond the garden was unfamiliar but as she stared at it she came to certain conclusions. She was not in London now, nor in any part of the suburbs, because there was no hum of constant traffic, though she

169

heard cars passing on a road nearby. From this she concluded she was at the back of some house near a road, but in the country. If only the sun...

The sky was clear, a pale blue-grey. Remembering it was now late October she knew sunrise would be late and low in the sky towards the south. If only...

It came at last; a clearer light, a burst of bird song and then long shafts of gold across the lawn. So she was right. She faced west or south-west. Then that faint blue line in the distance, a shape she half-remembered. Was it the South Downs? No, too smooth, too far off!

Thinking back to her Guide days she wetted a finger and pushed her hand out of the window. Yes, the wind came with the sun. That accounted for the fact that though the trees's branches stirred she stood sheltered at her window. Confirmation of her position, looking west.

She sniffed, telling herself country air would take away the pain that still shot through her head whenever she moved it from side to side. But the smell—the peculiar smell—the *recognisable* smell! An easterly or northerly wind, blowing to her the smell of Fawley oil refinery! She had breathed her fill of it that day with Roy on Southampton Water. It was unmistakable!

She stumbled away from the window and sat down on the bed. She must be at Overton, incredible as that might be! Kidnapped from Azalea Road, drugged to keep her quiet, unaware of her destination. Dr Phillips again, of course. With his thugs or just with Dr Waters? She remembered the swift skill of the injection into a vein of her arm. Dr Waters, practising anaesthetist, turned G.P. or just a highly accomplished junkie? She had seen them 'fix' themselves unerringly.

So they had brought her to Overton, where Roy was arranging a place for her after the funeral with the Mellishes or the Pratts. And this house was...?

She looked again at the window. Barred. Nursery bars. Not new, but strong. Had Dr Armitage had children, now grown up, or perhaps his predecessor? It had been a

170

doctor's house for donkeys' years, Roy had said. If this was indeed the Armitage house, then in another part of the building, in their separate flat, were Clare and Joe Pratt. Friends. If only...

She went again to the window. If only she could get a message to them. But how? She knew she had neither pen nor paper or any way of delivering a note that would not be intercepted. She could not be sure there was no watcher below at that very moment.

She tried to remember what Roy had said about Dr Armitage's household. He lived alone except for a disagreeable woman, his housekeeper. Again Lilian asked herself if he had been married, had children? Perhaps Roy had told her and she had not listened because she was hearing his voice, his much-loved voice, not the words he spoke.

Thinking about Roy would not help her, she decided. But then nothing she could do at the moment would help her. She was not absolutely sure that she was in Dr Armitage's house in Overton. In any case she could not imagine why she should have been taken away from London where she was supposed to be under police protection or so Commander Hull had implied. Police protection! She beat the window ledge in a rage.

While she was still puzzling and fuming over her present outrageous situation she heard a step on the stairs beyond the door and immediately leaped to her feet and darted behind it.

The key turned in the lock, the door opened and a woman went past her. Presumably the housekeeper, Lilian thought, as she saw a tray with food and coffee pot, two strong hands and then a wide back. The blankets and eiderdown that she had flung back towards the pillow when she sat down on the bed were humped up in such a way that anyone entering would not see at once that there was no one lying there. The woman was quietly approaching the bed table, not looking round.

In a second Lilian was outside the door, turning the key upon the intruder. Her heart was beating fast, she was

171

breathless from the sudden action and from excitement, she was dizzy from the last effects of the drug she had been given. But she was free.

Free from her immediate prison but not free of the house. As she turned with the key in her hand, as the woman inside the room raised her voice in a scream of rage and fright, a gentle voice behind her said, "You must give me that key, Miss Bartlett."

She recognised him at once. Dr Armitage, one of the two with Dr Phillips at Hamble, to whom Roy had introduced her. So she was not free at all. But she was right about where she was; where her prison was.

His voice was quiet, pleasant, a trained bedside voice, she recognised with a shudder for his betrayal of his profession. He was, however, not intimidating, just reasonable, soothing.

"Give me the key, Miss Bartlett. Mrs Hurst is becoming hysterical."

"Why have you brought me here? Where's Roy? What does all this mean? Are you mad?"

"The key, Miss Bartlett. Or must I take it from you?"

A fight, a struggle, would not help her, she knew. It would mean defeat and probably a fresh dose of unconsciousness. She handed him the key.

He went at once to the door to unlock it, saying as he moved past her, "There would be no point in running downstairs, Miss Bartlett. There are others who would stop you leaving the house, more roughly than you would like, I fear."

She did not move nor speak to him as he released a furious, tearful Mrs Hurst, who pushed past her so violently she shrank back against the wall of the narrow landing. Before Dr Armitage locked her in again he said in the same gentle voice, "You must eat your breakfast before it gets cold, Miss Bartlett. I will bring you lunch later on. This evening you will go with me on a little expedition."

"Where?" she asked, instantly afraid.

He disregarded the question.

172

"I must warn you that if you make any further attempts to get away, or to get in touch with—friends—it is only they who will suffer."

He did not mention Roy by name, but his meaning was perfectly clear.

"What you are doing is criminal," she said, knowing it was useless to threaten, but determined not to submit to open threats. "You can't keep me here, you must know that. Already I must have been missed. And I know . . ."

She checked herself, seeing his face harden and an evil gleam come into his eyes.

"Exactly," he said, moving now to the door. "You know too much, Miss Bartlett. Far too much. That is why we must keep you with us—for the present."

"For how long? My uncle's funeral . . ."

"It will all be taken care of," he told her. "You will not have to worry about that."

It came to her as the key was turned again in the lock that they were going to kill her when she had served some purpose, some diabolical purpose she might never discover.

All that day she sat by the window or lay on the bed. She drank the cold coffee on the breakfast tray and the water that Dr Armitage brought her with her lunch, which consisted of a plate of sandwiches. Being hungry by now she ate them all, noticing that the tray held neither knife, fork nor spoon. Not that she could use any of these to escape from her captivity or contrive to draw outside attention to her plight. She could throw the tray and the glass from her window, but only Mrs Hurst or the doctor would hear them fall and see the fragments.

In the evening, soon after dark, Dr Armitage came to her again. He ordered her to put on her top coat and follow him. When she asked where they were going he made no answer. A car was waiting in the drive. The doctor opened the rear door and told her to get in. The twe men inside moved to make room for her between them. She did not recognise their faces but thought the voices were familiar. Were they the thugs who had attacked

Roy or the masked men who had held her when she was kidnapped? It did not seem to matter now.

When the door was shut the engine and car lights on, the driver turned round in his seat. His face was in darkness, except for the dashboard light, but she knew him and her last hope faded.

"Good evening, Lilian," Dr Phillips said. "I hope you are a good sailor."

When Roy rang up Lilian just after ten on Tuesday evening he distinctly heard Dr Phillips's voice say, "Put that down, you fool!" before the receiver at the other end was slammed back, cutting off the call. If Phillips was speaking to Lilian and trying on his bullying ways again he wasn't going to win, Roy swore to himself. He waited ten minutes then tried again. The phone rang at the other end but no one answered it. He rang the practice number, but was told that calls had been transferred, this time to the number he knew belonged to Dr Phillips's house. He called the police at Scotland Yard, asking for Commander Hull. The commander was not available, he was told. There did not seem to be anything more he could do that night.

In the morning his work at the surgery held him until nearly eleven o'clock when he had his usual briefing from Dr Armitage and set out at once on his rounds. As he drove along the pleasant country roads between the coast of Southampton Water and the open Forest stretching towards Beaulieu and Lyndhurst, he once more felt his anxiety for Lilian rise to boiling point. He was so helpless, so tied down to his job, so overwhelmed by the double responsibility that had been thrust upon him.

On a straight stretch of road, still absorbed in his difficult problems, he was suddenly aware that a police motor cycle that had been following him sedately, suddenly swerved out, to run alongside, flagging him down.

Indignant, but puzzled, he drew in to the side of the road and waited. The patrol drew up in front, got off his bike and came back, removing one glove to fumble in his pocket.

"Dr Cartwright?" he asked, as Roy wound down the window.

"Yes. Have I done anything wrong?"

"No, sir. But I have to ask you to call at your early convenience at headquarters in Southampton to speak to Superintendent Coles. This morning, if possible, sir."

"Coles? But that's . . ."

"You'll find confirmation in the envelope."

The patrol went back to his machine, kicked it into action and was gone round the next corner before Roy had opened and read the brief official words. He looked at his list, then turned the car and headed back towards Totton.

Superintendent Coles was ready for him when he reached police headquarters just after noon. He lost no time in explaining that the reason for the call was to tell him about the latest moves at Azalea Road.

Roy was horrified.

"Taken away! But she was to have police protection!"

"She did. Chaps at the front of the house and at the way into the annexe car park. The front man saw a car draw up and three men get out of it and go into the house. One of them had a key to the door. The car was then driven round the corner and our second man saw it, empty except for the driver, go into the car park. About twenty minutes later he saw it drive out again, but now it seemed to have four people on board. He immediately checked with the first man and went off himself to report. Meanwhile one man left the house by the front door and walked away."

"Phillips, I suppose?" Roy said bitterly.

"I think not," Coles answered. "When the Yard got the report I went round to Azalea Road. No answer. So I went on to Dr Phillips's house. The doctor was still up writing his notes, he said. Miss Bartlett had been too upset by her uncle's death to perform her secretarial duties."

"Liar!" Roy broke in furiously. "Secretarial duties!"

"His own pompous words. He certainly had the National Health folders spread all around. He was very bland. He said he had been at home all the evening, since the end of the drug clinic. He intended to close this clinic, but it could not be done at once, only gradually, he told me. I asked him had he taken his car to the clinic and back? No, it was so near, he walked. He usually walked, unless he was going on to see a patient. Had he seen Miss Bartlett? Not since the afternoon, at the inquest on Dr Williams."

"That must have knocked him," Roy said. "Seeing I heard his voice in her house, not an hour before! As I tried to report last night."

"Then he must have been there. He simply looked a bit thoughtful. At that time I had not heard your report to the Yard. But he did say he understood Miss Bartlett had been advised to leave London for a time."

"Did he, indeed? Now who could have told him that? We dodged him when we left the coroner's court. He didn't even know we went to Scotland Yard."

"I'm afraid he did know."

"How?"

Superintendent Coles ignored this question also.

"You'll have to trust us, doctor," he said. "I can't say any more now. But I can promise you we'll have the whole thing cleared up very soon. You must help over this. Can you get away from your work this afternoon and evening? Particularly this evening."

Roy was astonished.

"I don't know that I can. Armitage has already told me he may not be able to take his evening surgery. Dr Thompson never does a Wednesday evening surgery, anyhow."

"I see." Coles's voice was hard. "Then it is more than ever important that you present yourself, preferably with oilskins or a thick jersey at Portsmouth Police headquarters not later than seven this evening."

"*Portsmouth?* Leaving this practice flat?"

"It'll be flatter than flat by tomorrow," the Superintendent told him. "But keep that under your hat. And everything else I've told you. Only turn up on the dot. I'm very serious. Miss Bartlett is in considerable danger. If we put a foot wrong anywhere we may lose her."

"But you seem to have lost her already! Or have you found her?"

He got no answer to this in spite of repeated entreaty and had to leave with his mind in confusion and his feelings driving him between rage and despair.

He spent the rest of that day visiting all those patients who were seriously ill, or just back home from hospital or just about to be admitted. Also a group of chronic cases that he thought would need renewal certificates for sickness benefit of one kind and another. As he knew well a great many poor folk, particularly the elderly, brought up to value thrift and independence, belonged to clubs and societies of various kinds that supplemented State benefits. Not only the better off with their private insurances displayed common sense and a healthy distrust of bureaucrats in power.

At seven o'clock he was met at Portsmouth headquarters by a police constable who, after identifying him, boarded his car and directed him to the waterside where he left it among others, all official and was taken to a powerful police launch. He was passed on board, again carefully checked. The rest of the complement seemed to be already there. Among them he was not altogether surprised to find Commander Hull, Superintendent Coles and a local Inspector North, captain of the launch.

Hull, after greeting Roy, went ashore again with the Superintendent, the vessel cast off and proceeded slowly towards the narrow entrance to Portsmouth Harbour.

"Come below, doctor," Inspector North said to Roy, "You'll want to put on that jersey. It'll be pretty parky outside."

Roy followed him into a warm cabin and while he discarded his jacket and put on both the jersey and an oilskin smock he heard the latest news.

"You know the position roughly, I think," the Inspector said. "An illegal immigrant racket, mostly Indians, poor devils, who are simply promised a great new life in England in exchange for their life savings. The lucky ones who escape this racket don't have any savings and are turned down and usually sent home free of charge—by us."

"Yes, I know all this," Roy answered. "Some of them managed the stowaway part of the operation, paid for in advance, then did the organisers out of the second payment for forged vouchers, passports and so on by melting away to the Midlands instead of reporting to Dr Armitage."

"Exactly. So the five left on board were taken off, not to be landed near Hythe, where they could get back into their own clothes and report in through the dock gates in the usual way, but on a useless raft off a lethal beach. Dead men tell no tales. Besides, they paid for the trip in cash to the syndicate."

"Syndicate? You mean Phillips and Waters and Williams in London and Armitage and Thompson down here."

"There were six, actually."

"That other London chap, Smith wasn't it, that died after a year at Azalea Road. Or Tom Markson? But they drowned him, didn't they? Or Mrs Hurst, the housekeeper? A six-man syndicate. A six-headed hydra!"

"A what?"

"Hydra. Little marine animal we meet in our first year biology. Old Greek monster with a lot of heads, that grew again as soon as you cut one off."

"Quite the Brain of Britain, aren't you?" said Inspector North, but he added thoughtfully, "Hydra. Very suitable. You had to cut them all off in one, I suppose, to defeat the habit?"

"Yes."

"We're having a shot now, doctor," North said. "But the trouble is they've got Miss Bartlett with them."

"Lilian! Oh, my God!"

"That's why you've been asked to come along. You

178

know the waters round here, don't you? The Nab, Selsey, Chichester Harbour."

"Pretty well, yes."

"Then I'll explain what we want you to do."

Lilian was taken on board Dr Thompson's motor cruiser and led down to the cabin, told to make herself comfortable and shut in, though she noticed that the cabin door was not locked. This was no relief to her, but in her shocked, confused and now hopeless frame of mind she felt too numbed to care. To find Dr Phillips down here meant that the gang was indeed giving up, making a getaway and because she had seen too much, knew too much, had betrayed her knowledge in many ways, she had to go, too. But not for long, she felt sure. Somewhere she would be discarded, somewhere in mid-Channel, too far off for any possible rescue.

And Roy? What would happen to Roy? She would certainly never see him again. He would soon forget her, though he loved her now. Her own love for him was deep, too deep to doubt him. It was indeed her only comfort in her present desperate situation. She prayed he might be made safe by her own death. She had no hope for herself. Leaning back on one of the bunks she shut her eyes, preparing for the end.

The cruiser cast off with the minimum of noise or fuss. Shaken out of her despair Lilian sat up. A light had been switched on in the cabin when she entered it. The long windows, not portholes, on either side, were hung with small curtains which she now pushed aside. To make her view from them clearer she found the cabin light switch and turned it off.

They were going down the river using the centre channel. The dark hulls of yachts on either side made shadows on the water which was bright from reflected shore lights. Many of the yachts were now squat shapes, their masts drawn out, their decks covered for the winter.

Soon they reached Southampton Water, glowing red

179

against the night sky, the tall chimneys at Fawley burning a flame at the summit, as in the daytime, but much more impressive now, she thought, against the night sky.

Then the motor cruiser slowed, swung round and as Lilian shrank back her view was cut by the hull of the fishing boat as Dr Thompson brought his cruiser along side. It was the old game she had watched with Roy. Or rather the expected sequel.

Jumping back from the bunk on which she had knelt to look out Lilian switched on the cabin light again. A second later the door opened and a procession of dark-skinned men in cotton clothes, one in a white turban, came down the steps, moving quickly but surely, hurried on from behind. As the last of them reached the cabin sole, Dr Armitage peered down.

"Miss Bartlett!" he called. "These men are cold. Will you please make coffee for them. And for yourself as well. You will find all you need in the lockers."

He was gone and in a few seconds the motor cruiser's powerful diesel engines revved up again and they were off once more.

"You would like some coffee?" Lilian asked, looking round at the eight figures who had seated themselves on the bunks, four on each side.

They nodded, so she began to search for cups or mugs and a kettle and some form of coffee and milk. She moved slowly, because now, as they left the shelter of the refinery and Calshot the swell outside grew and movement about the cabin became more difficult.

The man in the turban watched her for a few minutes, but when she had assembled what was needed and stacked it as well as she could in the galley, which was amidships, he got up and standing between her and the others said in a low voice, in very good English, "I can help you?"

He had a lighter in his hand, holding it out towards the calor gas stove. Below the lighter there was a folded piece of paper which he pushed into Lilian's hand as he withdrew his own from the stove.

"The loo is up forward," he said. "Read it there and destroy."

Lilian's despair fell from her; the hope, the courage that her hard upbringing had always found in her, surged back. She had not been abandoned.

Quickly, but very quietly, she made coffee, poured it into mugs, handed them round, keeping one for herself. She left this on the stove while she went forward and found the door she sought and locked herself in. There was a light switch here as well. She could read the note.

'When the Indians are put down into the dinghy you must go with them. You are to wear the turban. It will be given to you as you leave the cabin. Discard any distinctive clothing. Stay closely in the group. If detected, jump. You will be picked up.'

Lilian pumped the paper down the drain into the sea and returned to the cabin. She did not look at the man in the turban. She sat down on the opposite side of the cabin and drank her coffee.

The boat made rapid progress, the swell grew no worse. Lilian, with a sense of great relief, found she was not troubled by it. To be seasick in this crisis would be the end. Happily the sea was calm, but in its eternal fashion, far from still.

After nearly two hours the motor cruiser hove to, there were sounds of scrambling, short orders, the vessel listed, there was a heavy splash, she righted. The cabin door opened.

"Come on, you lot!" It was Dr Thompson who called this time, without looking down. "Lights out first!"

The order was obeyed instantly. Lilian felt her arm seized, the turban was jammed on to her head, a voice whispered, "Fasten the strap! Under your chin! Stay close to me!"

She obeyed, her excitement, her resolution, her defiance, rising all the time.

On deck, surrounded in a tight mass by the seven other Indians, her protector just behind her, Lilian saw that Dr

181

Armitage was crouched, holding a dinghy close in to the cruiser's side, while Dr Thompson was in the wheel house and Dr Phillips was at the after end of the cockpit, gazing alternately back towards the red glow of Portsmouth now some miles away and forward to a tall tower with a light on top, that seemed to Lilian to be dangerously close.

"Come on!" Dr Armitage urged. "Get down into the boat, the lot of you! We can't wait. Get down!"

They moved in a mass, quickly, neatly, as seamen should, including Lilian, who though not used to boats was naturally nimble and now very much afraid. Her friend, arriving just behind her, pushed her down to the floor boards, seized the turban and thrust it back on his own head. Lilian had not dared to look at Phillips after the first glance, in case she attracted his attention, but her guardian had seen the gun in his hand.

At the same moment that the Indians were all embarked, the 'put—put' of an outboard motor could be heard distantly, approaching from the direction of the dark tower.

Dr Thompson stuck his head out of the wheel house and yelled, "Let go! Get the bastards away!"

"There's someone coming!" Dr Armitage shouted back.

Thompson's answer was to rev up his engines, ready to move at once and quickly.

"Wait!" Dr Phillips cried. "There's one too many of them!"

He plunged into the cabin, shot up again.

"The girl!" he shouted. "They've got the girl with them!"

Armitage tried to hold back the dinghy but one Indian cut the painter with his knife, another slashed across the knuckles of the hand that tried to pull the dinghy close again. The little boat shot away, two men struggling to row it. Phillips levelled his gun at the turbaned head and fired. He guessed how Lilian must have escaped notice.

Immediately a powerful searchlight lit up the water, moved to the motor cruiser, held it in the beam, while a voice through a loud hailer ordered the owner to stop and wait for their arrival. A big launch, unlit until now, except for one light at a mast-head had approached undetected by Phillips, who had imagined it to be a fishing boat from Chichester or Selsey.

There was instant confusion. The rowing Indians, petrified, stopped, entangling their oars, nearly upsetting the dinghy, which was in any case taking water at an alarming rate. The outboard, cut off, allowed a second dinghy to draw in beside the other, when Roy's voice shouted, "Lil, Lil, where are you?"

Her answering voice was drowned in the noise of more firing. Phillips, beside himself with rage, fired again, at the police launch this time, aiming at the searchlight. An answering shot took his firing arm and he fell headlong into the sea. Another splash, another shout from Armitage and the motor cruiser made off in a smother of spray, while the police launch hove to, wildly trying to focus the searchlight on the spot where the cruiser had been.

In the water Roy, regretting his extra clothing, fought to hold up the now unconscious Dr Phillips until, having miraculously re-started its engine without trouble, the outboard dinghy retrieved them both and took them to the police launch, where Phillips was lifted on board while Roy, back in the dinghy was rushed over to the sinking craft they had meant to tow into Portsmouth.

"Lil!" Roy shouted again. "Lil, where are you?"

"Here!" she cried. "But this man was shot. I can't leave him."

"You do not leave us either," the Indians chattered piteously. "This rotten boat! We sink! We not swim!"

But the crew of the police launch had seen their predicament and moved along to pick them all up. There were seven frightened crew members of the liner *Antigone*, Roy Cartwright who had saved Phillips from drowning and Lilian, clinging to the folds of the turban she had wrapped as a tourniquet about the bleeding arm of the volunteer medical student who had risked his life to save her.

183

Chapter 18

At Portsmouth Dr Phillips was transferred to hospital under guard. With him went the medical student volunteer whose wounded arm, thanks to Lilian's First Aid treatment in the dinghy and that of Roy on the launch, needed only stitching and disinfecting. The turban, unwound from the underlying motor cycle helmet proved useful in dealing with both casualties.

Roy and Lilian, dried off, dosed with rum in hot coffee, were driven with Superintendent Coles to London and deposited at the Kensington house of Sir Henry Killick.

Roy had protested on the grounds that he could not leave the practice abandoned by its principals.

"That's been taken care of," the Superintendent told him as they drove away. He gave him the names of the doctors who had agreed to take all calls transferred to them.

"And the same has been arranged for Azalea Road," he added.

"Poor Uncle James," Lilian said. "But I'm glad he missed the show-down. It would have killed him."

"Instead of which he got out first," Roy said.

"No," she answered. "The suicide note was a forgery." She explained why she thought so.

"Dr Phillips murdered him," she said. "But I think it may not be proved."

Coles agreed to that.

"Not that it makes any difference in the end result," he said. "In fact a definite long sentence is better than 'life'. Keeps them out of the way longer."

"Why was Dr Williams in it at all?" Roy asked. "You did find out, didn't you, Lil?"

"Oh yes. It was in the diaries. He was doing very well

in his first practice, taking surgical cases into a local private nursing home. But he was already drinking too much, though his first wife was managing to keep it from the patients. She had an acute appendix. He refused to get anyone else to attend her and operated himself. He was drunk when he made the diagnosis and when he did the op. She died. He was nearly out of his mind. There was an inquest, a scandal, he was nearly struck off; would have been only the anaesthetist, Dr Waters . . ."

'The same Waters . . . ?"

"Yes, the same. He spoke for Uncle James—swore he was sober and that the death was from complications. Also the woman who acted as theatre sister, a former district nurse, called Tims, also gave evidence in his favour."

"You told me about her," Roy said. "She helped save him at the time, but he had to pay her blackmail from then on."

"Yes," sighed Lilian. "Blackmail was a big feature in poor Uncle James's career. Not from Dr Waters, though. He followed to be near Uncle James because he'd been under a bit of a cloud himself. Aunt Emily can't have known all this when she married him, but I'm sure she did later."

"He was very lucky in his wives," said the Superintendent. "Luckier than he deserved."

"He was a dear when he was sober," Lilian said sadly. "I think he might have got by if he hadn't been forced into this racket."

"One of the heads of that hydra, eh, doctor?" Coles said to Roy. Inspector North had told him what the young man had said.

"Yes. And Phillips was pulled in on account of his abortions at St Helen's before the new law. And the drug racket compromising them both, together with Waters. The same thing."

"It's a right mess," the Superintendent said, feelingly. "All these new laws. Comes of good intentions not allowing for ordinary natural human wickedness."

"Greed," said Lilian. "Greed must have got Armitage

185

and Thompson into this latest racket. And Mrs Hurst, I suppose."

They were silent, until Roy said, thoughtfully, "Mrs Hurst now. What's become of her?"

"Southampton pulled her in earlier this evening, boarding a train for London. She may have useful things to tell—useful details of times and such. Visitors to Armitage, coloured and white and . . ."

"Christ That reminds me . . . Yes, I'm almost sure! The time I went down to Overton and helped Clare across the road with the pram and young Jo and . . ."

"I think," Superintendent Coles said with a steady look, "you had better keep your recollections for Commander Hull. He might be very very interested."

At Heathrow a Mr Pullen lifted his two suitcases on to the weighing machine, offered his ticket to the girl at the desk and waited.

The flight had been booked some weeks ago; neither the date nor the time had been altered. A night flight to Pakistan.

This preliminary move over, freed from his luggage, Mr Pullen went to the bar for a drink, to the bookstall for a paper-back. He wondered if he should telephone again to Bernard, but decided against it. He would, he must, be well on his way by now. Also the others, their mission happily discharged. He smiled as that word 'discharged' came to him. A pity in a way. But no good pushing his luck too far. Luck? No. It was part of his genius.

Prepared and equipped for the flight, Mr Pullen approached the barrier passport open at the relevant page.

"Good evening, officer," he said pleasantly, recognising the man who held out a hand to receive it.

The officer did not answer. He looked at the page, he turned back to the front, inspected the photograph, lifted his eyes to his colleague on the other side of the narrow passage past the barrier. The latter stepped forward.

"I must ask you to come with me, Mr Markson," he said, smoothly.

Mr Pullen avoided letting out the gasp that seemed, inside him, to have blown off the top of his head. He said, gently puzzled, "My name is Pullen. My passport..."

"Yes," the officer said, still smooth and quiet. "But I must ask you to come with me."

Mr Pullen looked ahead. A policeman, unmistakeable, now stood in the doorway of the departure lounge. Behind, the queue of waiting passengers, a string of curious faces, beginning to show annoyance, stretched back some way.

"Very well," said Mr Pullen.

He held out his hand to the officer who still held his passport. It was given to him. He glanced at it. Yes, it was his all right. How could it be otherwise? Hadn't he burned...?

He made as if to put it back into his breast pocket but found his arm grasped and held. The officer said, "Shall I carry it for you?"

Mr Pullen surrendered. He let his hands fall to his sides as he was guided out of the queue, led aside through a door he had never noticed, into a corridor he did not know existed, to another door where two more airport police felt his jacket and trouser pockets, extracting from an inside one of the former a small round tube of pills.

"For air sickness," Mr Pullen protested. "Give them back at once."

He was disregarded. The door was opened and he was pushed, not roughly but with pressure he could not resist, inside a small bleak room. In front of him he saw, standing, Commander Hull and Superintendent Coles. Behind them, peering at him, white-faced, were Roy Cartwright and Lilian Bartlett.

"Mr Markson!" they both cried and repeated in the greatest astonishment, "Mr Markson!"

Mr Pullen, shaken now to the very depths of his being, still fought on.

"My name is Pullen," he said through dry lips. "I am a merchant in Bombay. I travel to England frequently. I am on my way back now. There is some mistake . . ."

"No," Commander Hull said. "No mistake. All you say is true, but since the day in September—check his passport, officer—that you left this country as Pullen, you have, by means of a forged passport in the name of Markson returned here, masquerading as that Mr Markson who was the father of Tom Markson, whom you murdered or caused to be murdered some three weeks before."

"No!" Mr Pullen still fought, but his voice had gone high and shook as he cried again, "No! I am Pullen! I have always worked in London and Bombay. Never in Southampton. I have never been there. Never in Overton. Never in my life!"

"Who said you had been in Southampton and Overton? Dr Cartwright!"

Roy stepped forward.

"This is the man I saw leave Dr Armitage's front door and walk to a parked car and drive away with an Indian beside him."

"You lie! You were not in Overton! You did not work there then!"

"Mr Markson, you are exposing yourself with every word you say," Superintendent Coles interrupted. "I warn you . . ."

Pullen collapsed. He had to be supported by the men on either side of him while Lilian identified him as the other guest at Roy's lunch party and the other man beside Mr Bourke at Scotland Yard on the afternoon of the inquest on her uncle. When she had finished he was led away, apparently a broken man.

"He'll probably put up a good defence," Commander Hull said when he had gone. "His enormous balloon of self-conceit has been pricked but he'll blow up another in time for his trial. He has a wonderful nerve. Calling himself Tom's father so that he was in everyone's confidence. Even coming into the Yard. He didn't know we'd

rumbled him weeks before and let him know our moves—
some of them—to flush his own. But he'll bob up again,
in spite of the evidence."

"Like those hydra heads you described, doctor," Coles
said, turning to Roy.

"No," Roy answered. "I think he is the body of the
hydra. The heads cut off were Dr Williams, deliberate, Dr
Phillips . . ."

"Recovering and chargeable," said Commander Hull.

"Dr Smith, who became an addict himself and died of
it," Lilian put in.

"Tom Markson, who was blackmailed on a frame, as
they tried to get me," Roy went on. "Same frame, same
crooks."

"Tom never wrote to his father," Coles explained, seeing
Lilian was about to protest. "Pullen was not his father.
Pullen is the partner in old Markson's firm. Old Markson
died over a month ago. Tom was in the racket all right.
From pity, I think, and anger at the discrimination he
found in this country."

"Not in the hospitals," Roy defended his profession.
"Usually not among patients either."

"But there all the same. Still, I think he did genuinely
want to go back and practice in his own country."

"Poor Tom," Lilian said. "We always liked him at
Azalea Road, Uncle James and I. And Gladdy."

"Who?"

"Mrs Gladstone. Poor Gladdy too. She wasn't in it, was
she? She's just grateful to Dr Phillips; always was, always
will be."

"We've nothing on her," Commander Hull said. "I only
hope we can make something definite stick on the others.
Pullen and Phillips, I mean. And Waters, of course. We
haven't forgotten him. Nor the crook lawyer, Ferguson.
The forger of vouchers and such. And the suicide note,
perhaps."

"What about Armitage and Thompson?" asked Roy.

"Nothing known up to date."

Nor thereafter. Nothing was ever heard of the Overton partners, though the motor cruiser was found on the rocks outside Cherbourg when the fog lifted on the French coast twenty-four hours later. However, the cruiser's rubber dinghy was still on board and after a search of the vessel a good sum of English money and some passports in a variety of names were found in the cabin. So it was considered they had not got ashore and must have fallen or been washed overboard when the cruiser missed the harbour entrance. Their bodies were not found.

Mr Bourke secured a copy of Aunt Emily's will from Somerset House. In it he found that the house in Azalea Road had belonged to her alone. She had bought it two years after her marriage. She had left it to Lilian, though Uncle James was to have the use of it during his lifetime.

Mr Bourke also discovered the whereabouts of Aunt Emily's brother, who had treated her so shabbily during her life time, in anger at her marriage to a drunkard with a past. This anger had extended to his niece, Lilian, and was not lifted by all the publicity she had to endure over the exposure of the two crooked, interlocked medical practices and their manipulator, the man Pullen, alias Markson.

"He is no loss to you, Miss Bartlett," Mr Bourke told her. "In fact his lack of interest is a gain, in a way. It has led us to a group of cousins who take a much more— modern view of your uncle and want to make your acquaintance."

Lilian was not impressed, though grateful. She would soon be married to Roy, when the Killicks and the Cartwrights would provide all the background family she needed.

As for Roy, he decided to forgive his Uncle Harry for getting him into the crook practices simply to help the law break them up.

"What if I'd let them blackmail me and gone bent myself?" he asked indignantly.

"I never even considered it," Sir Henry said.

"Or got put away by those devils?"

190

"That too I felt was unlikely."

"What *was* there in it for me? Did you ever think of that?"

"Experience, my boy. Valuable experience. Those *dregs* that everyone seems to love these days. Besides, you found Lilian. Wasn't that a lucky dip?"

"I'll say," Roy agreed.

"You better had," Lilian told him. "If you want me to be another of these unpaid, round the clock, telephone-tied helps that doctors' wives have to be."

"Not in a well-paid, well-run group practice, which is where we're going," he told her. "And as far from London, Scotland Yard and Uncle Harry as we can get."

"Are there group practices at Lands End or North Cape, then?" Lilian asked.